More than a story of children struggling to  school, this tale weaves in their family histc narrative of loss and dispossession that also gnant and heartbreaking, it is a story of reckoning with the past, while trying to navigate the present, in a world that does not understand.

—Fida Jiryis, *Stranger in My Own Land*

Alice Rothchild writes with deepest care and humanity, bringing the lives of children and Palestinian people into clear, delightful, honest focus. This engaging novel links generations with the verve and hope that has helped Palestinians—the "unchosen Semites" as a Jewish friend recently called us—survive so many hard, unfair times for so many years. We need more stories like this to balance the long injustices of tediously unbalanced reporting. It's a healing, joyous book of growth, and understanding.

—Naomi Shihab Nye, *Habibi, Sitti's Secrets, and The Turtle of Oman*

Old Enough to Know is a wonderful, heartbreaking and inspirational journey into the lives of a quirky 9-year-old American boy, Moham-med, and his Palestinian family who have just moved to a new home. As he learns to adjust to life in a smaller town, he begins to learn of his family's history in Palestine through his grandmother's stories. Through these stories, Alice Rothchild touches on so many of the tribulations that the Palestinian people face and have faced since 1948 (the loss of land and loved ones, oppression, the cycle of violence inside and outside the home, collective punishment, child imprisonment and other injus-tices). Rothchild provides us with relief from these tragic stories with humor and the strong vivid characters in Mohammed's life making this painful topic accessible to younger readers. This is a much needed story for young adults, parents and teachers alike.

—*Laila Taji, Founder of Arabish Way*

OLD ENOUGH
TO
KNOW

By
Alice Rothchild

Cune

Old Enough to Know

Library of Congress Control Number: 2023947505
Old enough to know
Rothchild, Alice, author.
Main title
Old enough to know / Alice Rothchild.
Published/Produced: Seattle : Cune Press, 2023.
Projected pub date: 2312
ISBN 9781951082840 (paperback)

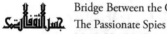

Bridge Between the Cultures (a series from Cune Press)	
The Passionate Spies	John Harte
Music Has No Boundaries	Rafiq Gangat
Arab Boy Delivered	Paul Aziz Zarou
Kivu	Frederic Hunter
Empower a Refugee	Patricia Martin Holt
Afghanistan and Beyond	Linda Sartor
Congo Prophet	Frederic Hunter
Stories My Father Told Me	Helen Zughaib, Elia Zughaib
Apartheid Is a Crime	Mats Svensson
Girl Fighters	Carolyn Han
White Carnations	Musa Rahum Abbas

 Cune Cune Press: www.cunepress.com

To the children of Aida Camp in Bethlehem,
who play, learn, create, and struggle
with the support of the Al-Rowwad Cultural and
Arts Society and the Lajee Center,
living the legacy of 1948 and the years that followed.

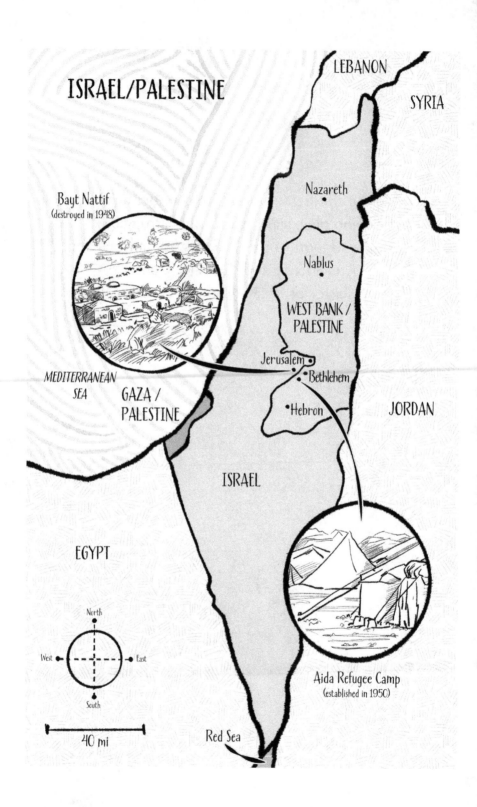

Family tree for Mohammed Omar Mohammed Abu Sour

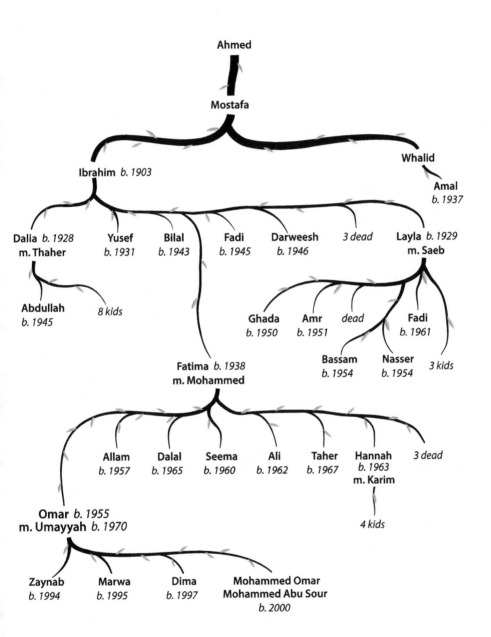

Ahmed

Mostafa

Ibrahim *b. 1903*

Whalid

Amal
b. 1937

Dalia *b. 1928*
m. Thaher

Yusef
b. 1931

Bilal
b. 1943

Fadi
b. 1945

Darweesh
b. 1946

3 dead

Layla *b. 1929*
m. Saeb

Abdullah
b. 1945

8 kids

Ghada
b. 1950

Amr
b. 1951

dead

Fadi
b. 1961

Bassam
b. 1954

Nasser
b. 1954

3 kids

Fatima *b. 1938*
m. Mohammed

Allam
b. 1957

Dalal
b. 1965

Seema
b. 1960

Ali
b. 1962

Taher
b. 1967

Hannah
b. 1963
m. Karim

3 dead

Omar *b. 1955*
m. Umayyah *b. 1970*

4 kids

Zaynab
b. 1994

Marwa
b. 1995

Dima
b. 1997

Mohammed Omar
Mohammed Abu Sour
b. 2000

OLD ENOUGH TO KNOW

MONDAY

Chapter One

Lost Tooth

MOHAMMED STARED DOWN AT HIS RED SNEAKERS AND BIT his pinkie fingernail. "Mom, I can do this myself. I am not a baby. I'm in fourth grade."

His mother called from the hall. "Wait for your sister."

He lifted his chin up high as if he was blowing his trumpet and strode down the front stairs, shaking his hips from side to side, his blue and gray backpack clunking each time a red sneaker hit another step, one shoelace already coming untied.

"I-will-find-a-friend," he chanted on each step. "I will blend-blend-blend."

His grandmother, his sitti, rushed out the front door. She tucked some stray hairs into her hijab, wiped her hands on her apron, and started waving. "Good luck habibi, darling."

Mohammed looked up and whispered. "Sitti, please go inside."

"Sweetheart, tonight I will cook your favorite chicken, just how you like it," she yelled. "You will be fine today. Maqluba, I promise."

His 16-year-old sister Zaynab, dashed down the stairs. "You think this is fun for me?" she glared. "I got better things to do on day one than drag you to school." She tucked her cell phone into the fold of her hijab, pressed it against her ear, and started jabbering with her old friend Monica.

Mohammed glanced back at his grandmother, then looked up and down the street. He spotted a lanky kid with a shock of hair hanging over his eyes, arms swinging loosely, striding quickly along the sidewalk. Mohammed's face reddened. "Please Sitti, pleease go inside."

Zaynab glared at him, "Oh, get over yourself. It's only chicken."

"But Zaynab, she's yelling…in Arabic…on our new street." Mohammed started walking, eyes glued to his shoes. He only looked up when the front door slammed.

He heard footsteps behind him and felt a new wave of anxiety. He turned quickly. "Hey, what's with the rag on your head?" sneered the kid, his pea green eyes peeking out of a mess of uncombed hair.

Zaynab stopped, whirled around angrily. She put her face inches from the boy's face and growled, "Get lost, jerk."

The boy looked up at her, scrunched his face, and spat, "Go back where you came from." He took off down the street, making whooping noises as he ran.

"Idiot! What the heck? What a neighborhood." Zaynab got back on her phone. "Monica, you won't believe what just happened."

The concrete buckled over a tree root and Mohammed nearly tripped and crashed into an overloaded black garbage can, bits of torn newspaper and old cat food cans piled on the ground.

"Look where you are going!" snapped Zaynab.

Mohammed jutted out his chin, squashed his lips together, and stared at her. The smell of old cat food drifted into his nose. *Stink-ee.* He nibbled on his nail and his mind drifted. *This is one rinky, dinky town.* He held his nose for a few seconds. *Not like Boston.*

He started thinking about his old school, his old buddies. *My luck Baba got a new job and we had to move to a whole new place.* Mohammed shook his head. *Right in the middle of summer.* His untied shoelace was getting looser and longer, dragging on the ground, picking up bits of leaves and crud.

Mohammed felt a sharp pain in his foot. He crouched to dump out a rock that was rattling around in his untied shoe. He picked off the dirt on his shoelace and tied a double knot. *Knot. Snot… Gross.* He glanced up at the cloudless sky. *Astronaut.* He pictured his face pressed against the window of a rocket ship, peering down from space at his new street, his new school, his grimy shoelaces, his annoying sister.

"Come on, hurry up," she said.

Mohammed stopped and shoved his hands in his pockets. His tongue wandered into an empty space, feeling his new tooth pushing up in the wide gap between front and back teeth. *I am M.I.A., missing in action.* He felt around his pocket. Empty. He hoped his silly putty was in his backpack. *I feel like a lost tooth in our big old smile.*

Mohammed laughed at that idea, all his old classmates like a row of teeth, just like the big grins in their class pictures. Charlie, Mohammed, Ali, side by side, arms around their shoulders. *Front teeth. Best friends since before I can remember and now this.* Maybe the tooth fairy, which he hadn't believed in for years, could just scoop him up and plop him back into that comfortable row of choppers.

"Hey, dream boy, take a left." Zaynab poked his shoulder.

Mohammed's stomach growled. At breakfast he had just stared at his oatmeal, too nervous to take a bite. He noticed the McDonalds across the street and thought, *an Egg McMuffin, now that would be a breakfast I could sink my teeth into.*

He heard his old teacher's nagging voice, "Mohammed, stop brooding and pay attention."

He played with that teacher word, "brood." It sounded kind of dark and stormy and it rhymed with mood...food. Food made him think about the lunch in his backpack, his favorite hummus and pita sandwich, and the stuff just jangling around in there.

"I've got quite the collection."

"Hey, are you talking to me?" Zaynab chuckled. "Monica, my brother is such a spaceshot."

"Spaceshot? You're from Ur-a-nus." Mohammed stretched out the end of the word. Zaynab shoved his shoulder. "Just shut up." Mohammed shoved back and sped up his pace, his shoes thudding on the sidewalk.

Last night he had carefully packed his backpack: his favorite Frisbee, a sampling of his bottle cap collection, (only 422 to go to get to 999), the red and white Lego pieces, Silly Putty from Charlie, and the soccer key chain from Ali. He missed his old friends. At least he still had his collections at home and the bits and pieces rattling around on his back, bumping against his lunch box.

"There's no real food at your school," his grandmother liked to say, stuffing the lunch box into his backpack. She was always in the kitchen, cooking food from "back home".

Mohammed smiled, imagining his crazy grandmother curled up in his backpack.

I feel like a snail lugging my treasures and my home on my back. That thought made Mohammed feel calmer, cutting into his first-day-at-school anxiety, like his old life was wrapped around his shoulders, supporting him and hugging him as he marched into the new life ahead.

Zaynab, grabbed his shoulders, "Look, toothless pumpkin face, you're here. At school. Go bother someone else."

Chapter Two

What's Wrong? Everything.

WHEN HE REACHED SCHOOL, MOHAMMED FOLLOWED THE SIGNS to his new class and wandered into his fourth-grade room. His heart thumped and drops of sweat collected across his forehead. He held tightly to the backpack strap like an anchor in a stormy sea, stopped, and gazed at the rows of desks.

His teacher greeted him at the door. "Welcome." She stared at her attendance list. "Let's see. I don't recognize you from last year. What is your name?"

"Mohammed."

"Welcome Mohammed. I'm Ms. Santana." She stuck out her hand. Mohammed fumbled to grab it. "You're in the right place. Put your stuff in the cubby over there and then just pick any seat for today, there's lots open."

Mohammed peeked at his favorite red Frisbee with the gold stars as he took out his water bottle. He picked out one of his bottle caps, a red Lego square, and the Silly Putty, and quickly shoved them into his pocket. As he tossed his backpack into the red cubby, he sniffed a fresh paint smell.

He wrinkled his nose and scanned the classroom, five rows of desks and a jumble of kids. He spotted a backpack just like his. The other fourth graders were chattering and laughing, stuffing their cubbies, scrambling for seats near their friends. Mohammed took a deep breath, exhaled quietly, and edged towards the other side of the room, close to the back. He placed his water bottle on a desk, feeling like he had just landed on some isolated island, and stared down at his shoes. Another pair of red sneakers bounced by.

He stood for a moment and glanced across the class, anxiously biting the nail on his pinkie. *I'm kind of a shy kid. Just the…lonely weirdo? What rhymes with that? Obviously nothing.*

Suddenly, a tall, lanky kid with pea green eyes and a shaggy mop of hair scooted up behind him and shoved him hard.

"Watch where you're going, jerko," the kid sneered.

"Hey, what?" Mohammed stumbled forward and caught himself on the edge of his desk. His water bottle teetered and toppled over, rolling onto the floor with a clunk as he stared at the boy striding towards the back row, high fiving his buddies. *Green eyes? Gees. Same kid this morning?*

Mohammed blushed a deep red, crouched to the floor, and reached for his water bottle. He noticed a crack in the plastic top. *My luck.* He groaned and squirmed into his seat. *I can't believe that moron is in my class.* He wriggled his head around, staring at the back-row boys. They were all blabbering and giggling loudly. In the front of the classroom, he saw multicolored letters dancing on the whiteboard:

> FOURTH GRADE TIGERS:
> Welcome to your new Community!
> Fourth grade tigers strive to be:
> EXPLORERS, CREATORS, SCIENTISTS,
> FRIENDS, & THINKERS!

Friends would be really great. Thinker-explorer-friends. Mohammed's best friends, Charlie and Ali, would be heading to school back in Boston. He could see Charlie's freckled face, his tangle of red hair creeping over his eyebrows, twisting around his big ears. And Ali, taller and thinner, with a goofy giggle that would throw the three of them into uncontrollable snorts of laughter.

He sighed. The three of them running back and forth on the soccer field. That was fun. After practice, tired and thirsty, they stopped for ice cream on their way home. *Chocolate chocolate chip, double scoop, three cones please.*

The clunk of backpacks joggled Mohammed back into the classroom. His heart made an extra thump when Ms. Santana walked away from the door and reached her desk. She looked around and said, "My friends, welcome back to school." She stuck both hands on her hips, accentuating the wide flare of her white and black checkered dress, and stared at the squirming students through her square red glasses.

A little friendly, a little scary, thought Mohammed raising his eyebrows and staring back at the teacher. He smiled. *She kinda looks like a checkerboard.*

"Some of you know each other from last year and some of you are new to this school. Today we are going to get to know everyone." Ms. Santana gazed across all the upturned faces and cracked the tiniest of smiles, crinkling her eyes together. Her hair was short and curly, the color of golden sand with patches of brown, bunched into a green clip on the side.

Kinda the same colors as my iguana. Mohammed tried to slow down his pounding heart by making up something ridiculous. *Iguana teacher. Teacher turning into iguana...iguana with red glasses. Iguana, banana...* He chuckled to himself until he heard his mother's voice. "Focus, focus."

A girl with black curly hair stared at him. "What are you laughing at?

Mohammed slunk deep into his chair.

Everyone settled down and there was a moment of quiet.

"Good. We are going to start with an icebreaker. When I call the roll," Ms. Santana said, opening her eyes extra wide for emphasis and tilting her head forward looking over her glasses, "I want you to tell us the scariest thing that happened during your summer vacation." She said "scariest" with a creepy wobble in her voice.

Most of the kids sat up straight and looked directly at her. Then she pushed her boxy red glasses back up the bridge of her nose and leaned back, perched on the front of her desk. "So, I visited my friends on Cape Cod and we swam in the Atlantic Ocean. The surf was really high and suddenly this gigantic wave came crashing over my head and knocked me over. My hands and feet went every which way and I thought I was going to drown!"

Several of the students giggled and the boy with green eyes yelled, "Did you get eaten by sharks?"

Mohammed felt a wave of nervousness rising in his chest. *Who is that kid anyway?* He grabbed a colored pencil, a piece of scrap paper, and doodled tight little circles, like springs ready to pop, surrounded by curling waves. He could hear the sounds in his head, *boing, boing, boing, crash, splash.*

He could see his teacher tossing in the waves, hands and feet up in the air, a scream on her face. *Scream…dream… team…* With his other hand, he reached for the Silly Putty he had put in his pocket. He just wanted to feel that smooth round egg in his hand, as if his old friend Charlie were actually sitting next to him. *A dream team.*

As opposed to his stupid sister Zaynab. Last night they had a fight. She teased him. Called the Silly Putty his "stupid transitional object".

"Whatever that means," Mohammed yelled back, knowing it didn't sound good, whatever it was.

"Not much better than sucking your thumb, baby, baby brother," she taunted.

"You're an idiot, you can't go anywhere without, without… your phone, that's a transitional whatever," Mohammed roared back, until his mother intervened.

"Kids, enough. Zaynab, please, you are much older than him. Be a mature young lady. Mohammed is nervous about his first day of school. Leave him alone."

Ms. Santana's commanding voice jolted Mohammed back into the classroom.

"Noah Bernstein?"

"Present. Went to summer camp and there were snakes in our bunk."

Oops, no brooding.

"Jacob Heart?"

"Yup. Awesome."

Ms. Santana cleared her throat and looked disapprovingly over the edge of her glasses. "Is that how we answer, Mr. Heart?"

"No miss, I mean, yes ma'am, I'm here." He slumped in his chair and closed his eyes with a smirk on his face. "I just stayed home and did nothin'." There was a loud guffaw from the front row.

"Jacob, this is the first day of school. We are all making our first impressions. Are you trying your best? Do you understand?"

Jacob opened one eye and stared at her, eyebrow raised. "Yes ma'am."

"Okaaaay. Next. Mia Heffernen?"

"Here. Got a puppy. And the first night I couldn't find her and she was hiding in my closet." A low murmur of approval swept across the class and one boy in the back row started growling and yipping. Mia threw back her curly black hair and smiled, then turned around and glared. "Those boys are such babies," she whispered as she peeked over at her best friend Emily.

Ms. Santana glanced towards the boys perched on the desks along the wall. They wiggled and shoved as if they were sitting on porcupine quills. "Boys, there are no dogs in this class. Please behave like fourth graders, you are not in kindergarten."

"I bet you were scared when you couldn't find your puppy. Emily Jones?"

"Good morning. I went to circus camp." She pretended to juggle and made a goofy clown face as Mia giggled. "Oh, yah, and a kid fell off the trapeze and broke her leg."

"Ouch, that must have hurt. Mohammed Omar Mohammed Abu?" Ms. Santana's voice trailed off in a big question mark. She stared momentarily at her attendance list.

Mohammed bit his fingernail anxiously, "It's Abu Srour, my last name is Abu Srour." He fidgeted uncomfortably in his seat; a flush of heat reddened his cheeks.

"Uh, uh, I, uh, moved. That was, uh, scary enough."

Everyone turned to stare. "Who are you? Why so many Mohammeds?" asked Seth, his blue eyes gazing intently at the new kid in class, as he wrinkled his nose.

"Hungry? What's with the nail biting?" snorted Jacob, sweeping his hand through a clump of long hair hanging in front of his face.

He squeezed his eyes together and glared at Mohammed.

"Where are you from anyway?" whispered Amelia, as she drew butterflies and flowers tumbling over a sheet of paper, her sparkly bracelets clanking against the desk. She tossed her head sideways as if hoping everyone would notice her butterfly earrings.

"I'm from…Boston," Mohammed Omar Mohammed Abu Srour blurted out quickly, shifting uncomfortably in his chair. He hated everyone looking at him. He shoved his hands under his bottom so he could not bite his nail. He had never felt so different before. No one had ever asked him those questions at school.

I wish I could go back to my old school with my old friends. His eyes filled with hot tears and he squeezed them together so no one could see. He tossed his thick black hair out of his face and slouched down at his desk. *Why? Why? Why?*

Ms. Santana stared briefly and said, "Sorry to have stumbled over your last name. You know, I have two middle names too and it can get confusing. Let's stick with your first name for now, okay. You are our only Mohammed." She smiled warmly, her eyes crinkling. "And yes, moving can be very stressful."

She finished with the roll. "Friends, the first day is always challenging." She put down her papers.

"Now, people. You are in fourth grade. That means listening, raising your hand if you have a question or comment. We are Fourth Grade Tigers. We are building a community in our classroom that is respectful and kind to each other."

Jacob bounced in his seat, clunking against his chair. Seth laughed and then slapped his hand across his mouth.

Ms. Santana stared at both of them with her I'm-in-charge-buddy, get–your-act-together look.

She sighed loudly and walked to a corner of the room and began pointing out the cubbies and bookshelves as Mohammed stared at the clock, waiting for each endless minute to flip forward. Suddenly, he felt something warm and furry brush against his leg. He stared. He jumped. "What the…!" He peered under his desk. *Of course, something awful always happens to me.*

Emily pointed and screamed, "A rat! It's a rat!" The kids scrambled up on their desks, a wave of screams and shrieks, knees clattering on wood.

Jacob yelled "Rat's looking for Mo. Sniff, sniff, Mr. Mo Hammed. Holy mogoly. So great. Evacuate, everyone evacuate the class."

All eyes on rat. No eyes on me. Mohammed crouched on his desk, literally chomping off his pinkie nail.

Amelia leaned over the desktop. "It's not a rat guys, it's a hamster." She clambered down and ran after the brown and white furry animal, cornering it against a bookshelf titled "Science in our Classroom. "Oh look, it's sooo cute. Come see."

Amelia scooped up the hamster and handed it to Ms. Santana who had rushed after her. "No need to panic, everyone back in their seats." The hamster bobbed her head and stared, nose twitching nervously. "Well guys, this is Shirley. She must have escaped from her cage. That's quite a way to meet her. Let's check that cage out right now."

Everyone swarmed around the hamster cage. "She musta' gnawed her way out the top," chirped Jacob, pointing at an irregular hole in the roof of the cage. "Wow. Wow. This is better than recess."

Ms. Santana plopped Shirley down and put a heavy book on top of the hole. Shirley frenetically scratched her ear and then dashed to the glass, stretching out her furry torso, grasping the smooth surface with tiny pink feet.

She's trying to get out again. Mohammed focused on being as invisible as possible. *Maybe I could escape like Shirley, maybe grab a bathroom pass and never come back.* The hamster made a squeaky chattering noise and burrowed deeply into her bedding.

Maybe I could hide like her. He imagined curling up in a big tub of wood chips, the teacher walking up and down the halls hopelessly calling his name. Mohammed Abu? He was not feeling like a tiger at all.

Chapter Three

Swiss Cheese

MOHAMMED'S MOTHER, WEARING JEANS AND A LOOSE GRAY BLOUSE, gave him a warm hug as he slammed the front door after school. For a second, his face got buried in her wavy, shoulder length hair. "My, my, you are getting taller. You okay? I was so worried when you left this morning. You didn't kiss me goodbye. How was your first day?" she asked.

"Could have been worse," Mohammed replied, giving her a don't-mother-me-so-much kind of look. Despite his pretty dreadful day, his mood briefly perked up as he caught the mouthwatering smells of chicken and spices.

His eyes scanned the cluttered living room, strewn with unpacked boxes, and the newly painted yellow kitchen where the afternoon sun was streaming through two large windows.

"*Maqluba*," he remembered his grandmother, his sitti, promised this morning. She was in the kitchen, bent over the stove, tossing sliced almonds into a pan of olive oil. Her hair was damp from the heat and she was wearing a loose print dress, wrapped in a pale green apron dappled with faded old stains from years of cooking.

Mohammed's 13-year-old sister Dima snuck up behind him and grabbed his waist as he crossed the living room, wrestling him to the floor. She bounced on his back, tickling his ribs and laughing as he struggled and squirmed to get up. "I got you this time. Now you can't get up," she teased.

"Get off me. You weigh a ton. You big elephant. Stop! Leave me alone!"

"Nope. Revenge little brother! Revenge! I've got you where I want you." She laughed triumphantly.

His 15-year-old sister Marwa, tall and muscular, walked into the room. "Okay you monkeys, that's enough." She pulled Dima off, let Mohammed go free, and tossed him a basketball. "Hey baby Mo, having a rough day? Wanna play?"

But Mother said, "No balls in the house, guys. Go outside."

In the corner of the living room, Zaynab was staring at her computer, earbuds in, her leg tapping to an inaudible tune, her mind deep into math equations. Her abundant curly black hair cascaded over her shoulders. She didn't notice her little brother standing and watching, frowning. *Maybe she's secretly a horse turned into a girl by some evil spell. I bet we're not even related.* Her cell phone was perched on her neatly folded purple hijab, next to a pack of gum and a small calculator.

Mohammed did not feel at all like going outside. *My sisters make me soooo crazy. Not fair. Outnumbered.* He imagined climbing hand-over-hand to the top of a very tall Lego tower, so high his siblings looked like bugs scurrying on the floor. Suddenly he lost his grip, falling, falling, landing with a thud amongst the unopened boxes in the living room. *Ouch.* He jumped at the thought.

I'm just going to be an invisible fourth grade weird nobody. Can't believe I almost cried. So embarrassing. Did anyone notice? Mohammed nibbled his fingernail. *All the other kids seem pretty normal, except that creep Jacob.* He crossed his eyes and growled, picturing Jacob surrounded by his back-of-the room buddies. *Of course, there is my endless name. It's not that I hate my name or anything, but…*

Ms. Santana's comment floated into his awareness: "You are our only Mohammed." *Who else in fourth grade is called Mo-ham-med?*

"Mom, why couldn't I be…Michael? Or…Mark? Matt?"

"Honey, Mohammed is a lovely name." His mother looked up from sorting the mail and shook her head.

"I feel so…weird, Mom."

Marwa shouted, "Spaceshot. You're holding the ball. How about we go outside?"

Mohammed shook his head. "No Mars, I wanna do some con-struc-tion." He bounced the ball with each syllable. He tossed it to Marwa and walked towards his bedroom where he could see his Lego project. He liked to pretend the tower on his dresser was his new apartment building and the desk was his old street. A red and yellow bridge let him go back and forth between his new and old lives.

Sold on old, old is gold, Mohammed thought. "Do you see what I'm building, Mars?" he said. "I got the whole street, here's our old house and the yard. Whaddayah think?"

"Really? You're the kid from Mars, baby bro. Why don't you try real life?" she asked as she bounced the ball out the door.

Maybe I should build a wizard fortress and go hide in it. He flashed on Shirley and The Great Escape.

His sitti looked up from her cooking. Her wire glasses slipped down the bridge of her nose.

"Habibi, sweetheart, come here. Sho malak?   What's wrong?" Her warm arms wrapped around his shoulders, and engulfed him in the smells of onion and sumac. As he looked up at her wrinkled face, his anger and anxiety faded and the tears gurgled up and started to flow. Mother always said they had a special bond because Sitti came to live with the family the same day he was born.

Sitti loved to tell how she left the crowded Aida Refugee Camp in Bethlehem and traveled in a dusty bus through the desert. With heart pounding, she got onto her first airplane in Jordan to fly across the ocean to meet her baby grandson.

They both arrived September 9th, Sitti from far away Palestine, Mohammed from the hospital in Boston.

Mohammed thought about the Egyptian mummies he learned of last year, with their big heads and rolled up bodies. *I remember the map, Palestine was somewhere out there across the Red Sea from Egypt. Close to Jordan? Not sure.* He had a very faint memory of an endless plane ride "home" back when he was a toddler. He loved to write that date: "9/9." His friends back in Boston told him that nine was his lucky number.

Sitti called her first day in America, "Our birthday." And she liked to tell stories. Mohammed suspected that all her talk was like Swiss cheese, tasty but filled with big holes. *What was life like before America?* He had heard that she lived in a refugee camp in Bethlehem, a place she called home, crowded into small apartments, piled together with other families. *But what happened in that camp? And why do I have such a weirdo name?*

Chapter Four

Mohammed Twice

Sitti handed Mohammed a tissue and he blew his nose loudly. "Sitti, why can't I be just Mohammed once?" he asked in a slightly gravelly voice, wiping his wet eyes with his sleeve.

"Ah, habibi, that's the problem. Let me start from the beginning." She patted his shoulder. "You know, since we moved this summer, I've been thinking a lot about my own moves many years ago, all the stories I didn't tell you."

"Waddya mean, didn't tell me?"

"I didn't want you to feel different from the other children."

"But Sitti, I am different." He blew his nose and pouted.

"Now, let me turn down the stove and then you come sit. I have something to say."

They curled up, snuggling into the soft cushions on the couch, pushing the red, yellow, and green embroidered pillows she had made into a pile. She crossed her legs and took a deep breath.

"Your name tells a story," she explained. "Your name is the way to remember your family, but you can't remember your family until you know our stories. Especially those I have kept from you."

"Kept from me?"

"It is time for you to know and to remember."

Mohammed looked up curiously; his dark brown eyes met her face. Her eyelashes were thick like his but had turned a silvery gray. They shared the same creamy brown skin, the color of toasted almonds.

"Mohammed is your name and Omar is your father's name and Mohammed is also your grandfather's name. Then your family name is Abu Srour, which means Father of Happiness. You are my happiness," she laughed.

"Mohammed is also the name of our prophet, peace be upon him, so it is an honor to carry that name."

Sitti's eyes twinkled. "It is our custom to use three names and the family name, but I could add your great-grandfather's name, Ibrahim, and your great-great-grandfather, Mostafa, and your great-great-great-grandfather, Ahmed. So, I could call you Mohammed Omar Mohammed Ibrahim Mostafa Ahmed."

Sitti laughed at Mohammed's wide-eyed look of astonishment. "And there's more. You know you call me Sitti which means grandmother in Arabic, but my first name is really Fatima, which is also the name of the daughter of the prophet Mohammed, peace be upon him. So we both have very meaningful names."

Mother stood in the door and added, "Your father's first name is Omar so some people call Sitti, Um Omar, the Mother of Omar. Our names are all about our connections," she smiled.

Mohammed tried to imagine people calling his mom Um Mohammed, and started to laugh. *So not happening here.*

His sister looked up from her computer. "If you think you're strange, baby brother, think about me: Zaynab Omar Mohammed Abu Srour. My middle names aren't even girl's names and they are obviously Arabic. Throw in the hijab and kids yell and call me a terrorist."

Mohammed flashed on the walk to school this morning. "Like that kid who tortured you?"

Sitti shook her head, her eyes scrunched closed with worry. "Yah. Duh. Like lots of kids. What planet do you live on?"

Their mother continued. "Come on Zaynab. Mohammed, sometimes instead of our family name, we even use the name of the village near Jerusalem where our families came from long before we moved to America, so you could be Mohammed Omar Mohammed Nattifi, a boy from Nattif."

"But Mama, if you can put in Nattif, why can't you take out a Mohammed?"

He grew serious, a puzzled expression on his face. He briefly stared at Zaynab and shrugged his shoulders. "Mama, Nattif? Really? You always said I'm from Boston. I've never left the country for more than a week or two. How could I be from Nattif?"

"Ah, that is a long story for another day. I need to help Sitti get ready for dinner."

This is such a puzzle. Why are people keeping confusing secrets? What are they hiding? Mohammed picked up one of Sitti's embroidered pillows and traced the designs with his finger, like a miniature maze for Shirley. *At school I'm only a lonely... what?* He imagined himself floating in a blimp high in the clouds above his school with MOHAMMED MOHAMMED printed across the bulging silver belly, Zaynab's blimp floating above him. At *the same time, I'm kind of a somebody at home. Maybe, maybe my sister is related after all.*

A new intriguing connection was growing inside of him. His name meant he could not forget where he came from. But where exactly was that? And how was he going to survive another day at school as the strangest new kid in history?

TUESDAY

Chapter Five

Salami Jerk

THE NEXT DAY, MOHAMMED DRAGGED HIMSELF BACK TO SCHOOL, happy to be free of Zaynab. *Stubborn as a mule in school.* He smiled at the idea of a mule trotting into class and slid into his desk next to Noah who was lost in his Marvel Comic book. Mohammed stared at the yellow cardboard nametag taped to the shiny surface of his desk. He had followed the instructions yesterday to write his name in his very best handwriting: MY NAME IS MOHAMMED OMAR MOHAMMED ABU SROUR. *At least I didn't add Ibrahim Mostafa Ahmed. That would kill me.*

Noah was wearing a baseball cap and tapping repeatedly on his desk with a ruler, oblivious to the annoying sound he was making. The other kids chattered. Jacob and Seth pushed each other, landing on the floor in a tangle of elbows and knees. Mia and Emily giggled over a photo of Mia's new puppy sitting in a basket.

Emily was wearing a red clown nose, goofing and laughing until Ms. Santana cleared her throat and said, "Friends. Listen up. Now. Get up off the floor!" Almost everyone scrambled to their seats and there was the clatter of books hitting desks, papers rustling, chairs scraping. Jacob sauntered over to the pencil sharpener as if he had all the time in the world.

Mohammed stared at Jacob's empty seat in the desk across from his. *My luck. He's at my table group. Torture.*

Ms. Santana stared over her glasses and said sternly, "Jacob Heart, wipe that smirk off your face and sit down now."

Mohammed gazed at the red digital clock on the wall, wondering if time slowed down when school started. A science experiment was laid out on the desks, rows of white paper cups, and on the white flip sheet Ms. Santana had written: Observations and Inferences: Use your four senses (not taste, this is science) to observe the mystery substances. What can you infer about the data you collect?

Mohammed daydreamed about the stuff in his backpack collection and the stories he was collecting from his sitti. *It's all data. What's that word the teacher used?* He looked up at the flip sheet. *Oh, infer. What can I infer from my data?* He rolled his mouth around the "R" while staring at Noah. "Inferrrrr."

Noah startled, suddenly aware of Mohammed.

Noah shoved his comic book under his desk. "Hey. You're the new kid?"

Mohammed responded, "Yeah. I'm the one who just moved, remember." *Just what the class needs. Another disconnect from reality like me.*

Jacob slid a piece of paper onto Mohammed's desk. Mohammed stared at the scrawled letters. WIERDO.!!! GOTTA

BOMB IN THAT BACKPACK??? Jacob grinned. *Idiot. He can't even spell weirdo… data coming in. REALLY bad day ahead.*

At lunchtime Mohammed sat by himself and listened to the crackling of unwrapping sandwiches, tuna fish and chicken, and a flat bright orange cheese tucked between slices of white bread. He spotted Oreo cookies, chocolate granola bars, and licorice sticks. Jacob was chomping noisily on a salami sandwich with mustard and slurping on a lemonade juice box.

Cautiously, Mohammed peered into his lunch box, dreading the familiar thin pita bread with hummus, a dense sprinkle of za'atar, and olive oil leaking from the top, a plastic container filled with tomato and cucumber chopped into tiny pieces dripping with lemon juice, and a sack of salty pistachio nuts. This was what his sitti called, "A real lunch for a growing young man."

At his old school, all his friends brought lunches from home. He and Ali often laughed at the similarities in their food. Ali used to slap him on his back and joke, "Hey Mohammed, we're friends through thick and thin, hummus to olive oil." That didn't feel so funny now.

Jacob got up, his lanky frame unfolding like the beams of an Erector Set, swatted his rambunctious hair back, and ambled by. "Whatcha eating Mo? A dirt sandwich?" He sneered, chuckled, and bounced over to a cluster of boys. "Is that some kind of A-rab food?" They all turned and stared at Mohammed, laughing and grunting, "Gross, gross, gross," and pretend smacking their lips.

Stupid apes. Mohammed stared at the hummus. Sitti in the kitchen crushing the chickpeas, mashing them into the thick sesame seed paste, squeezing a lemon and crushed garlic into the mix, and thinning it all with a drizzle of olive oil. The za'atar too. She toasted sesame seeds and added that to thyme and oregano with a big dollop of sumac and coarse salt. When she cooked, Mohammed loved the smells wafting out of the kitchen.

"Like home," Sitti sighed and then always added, "But the thyme is not exactly the same and of course the olive oil is not from our village, so…almost like home."

Noah came by and sat down, his thick black hair poking out in all sorts of crazy directions from under his baseball cap. When Mohammed looked up at him Noah said, "Jacob used to torture me last year. Don't pay any attention to those guys. Jacob is a jerk. A real big jerk. A salami jerk."

Mohammed looked cautiously at his new classmate and laughed.

"I hate lunch," Noah said. "My mom is Chinese and some-times she makes food that is just too weird for school, like, like…" He rolled his eyes, "Like spicy tofu with tons of scal-lions. For school. And then she packs chopsticks too. No way. I just leave it all in my locker and dump it in the trash before I go home." Noah gave him an understanding glance.

Mohammed smiled and nodded cautiously. He didn't know what tofu was, but it sounded pretty strange. "Don't you get hungry? What if your mom found out?" he asked and nibbled his fingernail.

"I just buy a hot dog and cookies from the cafeteria with my allowance," Noah asserted with confidence, like a kid who had figured out all the home and school lunchtime landmines. "She won't find out. I bring the chopsticks home with a little food stuck on them to be sure. Kinda swirl them around before I dump the stuff in the garbage. So, she always thinks I ate her lunch. Beats torment in the cafeteria."

Well that's one fine solution, but I couldn't throw Sitti's food away. No way. Mohammed stared at Noah's hot dog. *I just need to get through lunch and band practice and math, and if I haven't been made into a salami, then I need to get out of here.* He looked at Noah again and said, "It sure looks easier to chomp on some salami than have hummus and olive oil dripping down my fingers."

Noah turned to him, "Yeah, but you got that black stuff stuck to your chin." Mohammed didn't know whether to laugh or cry, but Noah handed him his napkin and started to laugh. Mohammed felt a chuckle growing in his belly, rising up in his chest, and let out a loud guffaw. Soon, they almost fell on the floor poking each other and bursting into giggles.

During band practice, everyone turned around as Emily crashed the cymbals together at the end of Hot Cross Buns. Mohammed smiled, his lips tingling from his efforts to make a good trumpet sound. He had not played all summer and was feeling a little rusty. He wiggled his lips, trying to restore some feeling in them. He tightened his mouth and exhaled a loud vibrating raspberry. Mohammed sat behind Seth who was struggling with his clarinet and Noah who was curled around a French horn. In front of them, Amelia tooted cheerfully on her flute. There were rows of black music stands, an old upright piano in the corner, and a big bass drum next to Emily.

The band conductor waved his arms rhythmically around in front of the students, undaunted by the jangling noise. He popped his baton behind his ear and said, "Okay, good first try. I want everyone to practice this piece ten minutes every day and write it in your practice log. Let's do it again from the top. Work on keeping a steady tempo, watch my hands. Okay. One-two-ready-go."

There was an audible inhale as the kids started again, a clatter of chirping and blaring, everyone intensely staring at their music. Mohammed tried to focus. His new word from class, *embouchure* floated into his brain. That's what the band teacher called the puckering of his lips to create the trumpet sound. He also liked this new word *tempo*. He counted in his head and tapped his foot to the beat.

He loved the swirl of blasts and tweets and bonks around him and that feeling of being part of something, even if that something sounded a little chaotic.

After practice, Amelia said to Mohammed, "That was fun. We needed more trumpets." Mohammed smiled shyly back when suddenly Seth whacked him across the shoulders. "Good job bro'. Welcome to band."

Chapter Six

Big Questions

MOHAMMED RACED HOME FROM SCHOOL, HIS EAR BUDS DANGLING from his pocket and his face in a worried frown. He ran down the hard, concrete sidewalk, past the red brick apartment buildings, up the stairs, and found Sitti in the kitchen simmering fava beans, chopping parsley and mint. He dropped his book bag and his trumpet and rushed to his room.

"Don't leave your jacket on the floor," his mother called.

As he flopped on the bed, he stretched out on his back. *What a gonzo day.* It was a little smoother than yesterday, but there was that awful Jacob. The teacher smiled at him and asked him to pass out the math problems. Seth invited him to shoot hoops during recess, Mia shared her markers when they were drawing the different parts of plants, and Noah sat next to him at lunch. *Awesome, possum,* he grinned a bit. No one mentioned his name, but something was still bothering him.

He stuck his head under his pillow, closed his eyes, and wrapped his arms around the soft blue iguana cover. He felt the pillow pressure on his eyeballs and his mind drifted. Suddenly he felt hungry for something. *For what?*

Sitti knocked softly on his door and peeked in. She crinkled up her nose and tilted her head with a worried look.

Mohammed always said hello when he came home from school and he never flopped on his bed in the middle of the afternoon.

Quietly she opened the door, carrying a bowl of tightly rolled grape leaves stuffed with rice, stacked like little green cigars, and a plate of sweet baklava dripping with honey.

"Eat habibi, you will feel better. I rolled the grape leaves this morning."

Mohammed peeked out from under his pillow and stared at the bowl and the plate. Suddenly he understood what was troubling him. He thought about the hot dogs and chocolate chip cookies they served in the cafeteria. He knew they never made stuffed grape leaves or baklava at school and his sitti had never tasted a hot dog. He could just imagine Jacob's snarling comment, "What's that, weirdo? You eatin' green dog poop?"

Sitti placed the food on his dresser, sat down on the bed, and gently rubbed his shoulders. Mohammed squirmed and turned to face his grandmother.

"Sitti, I love your food, but I...I...I just can't take it to my new school. It's, it's, like it's different here," he stammered, afraid of hurting her feelings.

His grandmother shook her head. "Sweetheart, this is not like you. What's going on? Did something happen at school today? Did a kid say something mean? What's bothering you?"

Mohammed squinted reluctantly at Sitti. "Well, there is this awful jerk named Jacob and..." Slowly the story about the dirt sandwich spilled out of him like a wave building and crashing on the shore with a loud swoosh, little bubbles of foam sinking into the sand. He could see each bubble pop like a smirking mouth. Jacob's mouth.

Sitti raised one eyebrow and stared at her grandson. "Your name, what we eat. It is much more than hummus and pita bread and some mean boy at school. This, Mohammed, is about who we are."

Mohammed rolled the pillow against the wall and sat up, giving Sitti a curious look. He had never seen her appear so serious. "You mean, like what mama was saying about where we are from? You know, I really didn't get that. Where's Nattif? How can I be from there?"

Sitti stood up and reached for the bowl and the plate and held them in front of Mohammed's face. "Eat."

"But Sitti, I don't..." Mohammed looked down at the plate and heard a loud grumble from his stomach. He swung his legs to the floor and picked up a stuffed grape leaf from the pile, took a bite, a dribble of olive oil and lemon juice curled down his chin.

Sitti said, "Come. Let me show you something. I have been waiting for you to ask." She patted his chin with her handkerchief. Mohammed reluctantly followed her and the grape leaves and the baklava out of his room and into hers. He breathed in her lemony garlic scent and stared as she opened the bottom drawer of her dresser.

Suddenly, Zaynab burst into the room, her eyes red from crying. She was gripping her torn hijab.

"Sitti, I can't stand this place. I was walking back from school, and, and...I hate this thing!" Zaynab threw her ripped scarf on the floor. "Why am I wearing it? Ughhhh!" She groaned and clenched her teeth in frustration.

"Habibti, let me give you a hug. Was it that boy from yesterday?"

"No, no. Two girls, they just ran up behind me out of nowhere and grabbed my hijab, and they were laughing and yelling 'ISIS! Suicide bomber! Terrorist!' And the other kids just stared and, and…laughed. Oh Sitti, it was so terrible."

Mohammed felt a pang of sympathy. "But Zaynab, you're always so tough and…"

"Baby brother, I am so tired of being tough. Kids see my hijab and I'm like, like everything they're afraid of or they hear about, I don't know, on TV or their stupid cell phones."

"Come sit. That was awful and scary, my poor darling," said Sitti.

Zaynab took the tissue from Sitti and blew her nose. She wiped her eyes and blew again. "I can't sit. I'm too freaked out."

"But Zaynab," Mohammed started.

"No one sees me, ME, just a regular American girl. I mean, I want to go to college, I want a boyfriend. I want to be an engineer, just like dad, I…"

"But, do you really want to wear your hijab?" asked Mohammed.

Zaynab sighed loudly and rolled her eyes. "Look Mohammed, I wear this thing to be a good Muslim girl and that's why I'm supposed to wear it. Get it? And Baba says it is God's will, but I just don't know if I can take this. Not if kids torment me."

"It is God's will. It's part of the Quran, to be modest, to cover your hair," Sitti said gently.

"I know. I know." Zaynab threw her hands up and looked at the ceiling. She took a deep breath and then stopped.

"You know, putting on the hijab was actually…a relief." She half smiled.

"A relief?" asked Mohammed.

"Yeah. On a bad hair day there is nothing better than a hijab. My hair is so thick, so curly, so crazy to tame every morning. You know, a girl is supposed to have silky, straight hair and…"

"Don't know anything about girls' hair," mumbled Mohammed.

"Trust me, life got a lot easier, getting dressed and getting out of here in the morning, but then…I have to go outside. I didn't sign up for all this, this…"

"Hatred," said Sitti quietly.

"Yeah, hatred and stupidness," answered Zaynab softly.

"Of course not. Go wash your face and come back here. And eat something. You need to hear this too."

"Hear what?" Zaynab asked.

"Just listen to me," Sitti said.

When Zaynab returned, Sitti handed her a piece of sticky baklava. "Eat," she said firmly. Zaynab took a bite. "You and Mohammed, see what you can find." She pointed to the open drawer and stepped back, arms folded across her chest. Mohammed tilted his head and looked at her with his eyebrows raised.

Under a collection of folded scarves, Mohammed felt a large iron key, darkened and rough. It was very different from the shiny key that opened his front door. He handed it to his sister.

Sitti wrapped her arms around both of them and said, "Habayyeb, sweethearts, I have so many stories to tell you, stories I want you to remember, stories about Palestine, my home and your home."

How could it be my home? Mohammed wiggled uneasily.

"I want you to see where you come from. You know, now that you have moved from Boston, we all have left places and people, just about everybody and everything we know and love. It's hard. Right?"

"Right," answered Mohammed, feeling slightly bewildered.

"Sitti, what does this have to do with my torn hijab?" asked Zaynab impatiently. "I've really got so much homework to do and I'm supposed to call Monica before dinner."

"This is more important. Follow me," Sitti answered.

"But Sitti!"

She grabbed Zaynab's hand and walked towards the living room. "Sit." They settled into the soft cushions on the couch. Afternoon light streamed through the window. Sitti began to speak.

"Let's start with the key. This key opened the front door of my parent's home."

"Really, Sitti?" Zaynab asked. "It looks like it's a hundred years old."

"Hold that heavy key and it will unlock the memories I carried across the ocean. We had a beautiful house in Nattif, a little village just southwest of Jerusalem, and you're right, that key is very old."

"The Nattif Mama was talking about?" Mohammed felt the weight of the key in his palm and handed it back to Zaynab who curled her feet under her legs and leaned back on the couch, sighing loudly. "What can the past have to do with me? Now?"

Mohammed wiggled against the embroidered pillows. They both stared at their grandmother's face and wondered about the strange look in her eyes.

Chapter Seven

Sitti's Story: Bayt Nattif – 1943

"**W**AIT FOR ME." FIVE-YEAR-OLD FATIMA RUNS AFTER HER brother Yusef as he bounces up the stony road, riding bareback, his legs wrapped tightly around the donkey. They are both dwarfed by a tower of wheat tied in wide sheaves roped across the donkey's brown back. The donkey's belly bulges slightly. Fatima's loose gray dress blows against her legs as a breeze gusts up from the valley. Her two tight pigtails flop as she darts and dances around the trotting animal, waving her straw doll with the raggedy red skirt. She loves the donkey's deep brown eyes and over-sized ears.

"Donkey, donkey. What do you see? What do you hear? Tell me, tell me," she chants playfully, her bare feet skipping between the white stones jutting up from the path.

"Yusef, Yusef, when is the baby coming?" she asks as she runs along the donkey's side, reaching to pat her bulging flank.

"It takes a long time, maybe after the olive harvest," replies Yusef.

Fatima thinks back to that early morning in the field when the neighbor's donkey came trotting over. She heard all the braying and snorting. "So much noise to make a baby," she exclaims.

Her eyes catch a sudden glint of metal in the pathway. "What's that Yusef?" asks Fatima pointing.

"It's a gift from the British, a stray bullet," replies Yusef.

Fatima crouches to examine the metal fragment, frowning as she touches its' shiny surface. Suddenly she feels afraid. "A bullet?"

Yusef yells, "Fatima, just throw it as far as you can. I don't want to see it."

She hurls the tiny bullet, watching it bounce down the stony hillside. Her eyes scan the brown dry grass and rolling hills beyond and the big, cloudless sky.

Suddenly her cousin Amal charges towards her, "Catch me, catch me if you can."

"Oh no, I'm faster than you," says Fatima and she dashes up the road after her, giggling. "Faster, faster."

They are followed by a parade of sisters and brothers and cousins, the older boys carrying massive sheaves of wheat balanced on their heads. The sheaves are tightly roped together, loose ends shooting every which way and leaving a trail of golden stalks. They come to another path and see two older girls coming up from the cistern in the valley below, holding hands. They are walking ram-rod straight, large clay water jugs balanced on their heads. Layla's hair is tucked into a floral kerchief but Dalia's flowing white head scarf billows in the breeze.

"Look. Are you going to fly like a bird?" Fatima yells, pointing at her sister. She puts her doll on her head and tries walking ever so slowly, neck straight, flapping her arms.

Her sister half smiles. "You are so annoying."

As the doll tumbles to the ground, Fatima moves toward her sister but doesn't dare give her an exasperated shove. If the water jug toppled, or even worse, broke into pieces, she would be in big trouble, very big trouble.

Fatima turns and marches ahead. The donkey's hoofs clomp rhythmically as they all zigzag their way up the hill, laughing, teasing, and hugging each other on their way to the mill and then home.

An aunt in a loose, blue dress, embroidery on her sleeves and neckline, a wide belt bunching the cloth at her waist, passes the children. Her long white headscarf ripples slightly. "As-salaam 'alaykum, peace be upon you," she smiles. She barely nods as she balances a wide, flat, woven basket on her head piled with just-picked fragrant thyme and leafy greens.

"Wa-alaykum salaam, and upon you peace," the parade of children responds in an uneven chorus.

Fatima stops and turns to look down the hill where her father and uncles are bent forward. They are sweeping their sickles back and forth, cutting the wheat with the other fellahin, peasants from the village. The wind gusts and a golden wave arcs across the field. She inhales the crisp, dusty smell of freshly cut dry stalks. Beyond that, she can see the stubble of the barley harvested earlier when the spring rains stopped.

"And what is beyond that?" she asks, scrunching her thick eyebrows together. Her aunt pauses and says, "Habibti, face the sunset. Then if you keep hopping and dancing like that, you will get to the white beaches of Gaza and the blue Mediterranean Sea and then who knows."

Fatima closes her eyes and tries to imagine the sea, water like the rippling wheat and barley rolling along the valley. But water, so much water. She opens her eyes hopefully, but the lowlands are still there and her feet are still dusty and dry.

"Oh, I want to touch the sea," she exclaims. She whirls around and the rolling Hebron Hills stare back at her, dotted with silvery olive trees and clumps of towering saber cactuses. She waves at the cactuses with their thousands of prickly green mittens popping out in all directions.

An old man with a cane and a sun wrinkled face walks towards her, rolling his prayer beads with his knobby fingers. "Child, who are you waving at?" he asks. His face is framed by a white keffiyeh, his eyes watering from years of hot sun and dry dust.

"Uncle, everything that is alive is my friend," Fatima replies and he smiles, tugging one of her pigtails.

"Habibti, you are a curious one. Always with your stories." The call to prayer echoes in the air, the tall white minaret in the distance poking up at the sky from the white dome of the mosque. "Aye, so late already. I must get home to wash and pray."

Fatima loves the predictable rhythms in her life, the muezzin's call to prayer five times each day, the daily feeding of chickens and baking bread, the planting and harvesting each season. The babies bundled in blankets, growing and getting bigger just like her. Already she is thinking about Eid al Fitr. Last year at the end of Ramadan, there were family visits and feasting, special sweet dates, the hearty smells of roasting sheep.

"When will Eid come?" she tugs at her brother's shirt. "Ahh, I think after the olive harvest, when the baby donkey is here." Harvest. The tarps and blankets spread under each olive tree, the ladder her brothers and father climbed to beat the branches, the olives raining down, tap tapping in higher and higher piles. In the middle of the day, the entire family stopped and sat under the trees, eating tasty maqluba. The younger children chased each other from tree to tree.

"This year will I be tall enough to reach the branches?" she asks.

Fatima twirls around and around, wrapped in her five-year-old thoughts. Suddenly she realizes that Yusef is already at the top of the ridge. Fatima doesn't care. She has reached one of her favorite places in the village. She can already see the tall, cream colored column, cracked and rough with age, standing watch over the ancient site. Fatima climbs over a collection of large boulders, her dress catching on the dry twigs, her legs protected by baggy blue trousers. She hoists herself up on one of the jumble of tumbled horizontal columns and walks, heel-toe, heel-toe, to the end and jumps down.

"Where are those tiles?" she says to herself. Her toes scrape the ground, pushing the sand away until bits of blue and red mosaic appear. Impatient, she gets down on her knees and uses her hands to expose more of the tiny square mosaic pieces.

Yusef had told her, "These are really old, from the Roman times." She sits and stares, trying to imagine what stories the tiles could tell.

Fatima scrapes more of the sand and starts digging with her hands under one of the fallen columns. "Maybe I will find a really old coin," she says hopefully.

She jumps when she hears the sudden loud bleating of sheep and goats that have wandered between the columns and flat stones near the old road. She looks at one of the sheep, chewing a wad of grass, staring back at her as if to say, "What are you doing here?"

"I live here," she answers.

Mama's probably getting worried. Fatima scrambles back to the road, passing terraces and rows of thickly twisted olive trees, stones tucked into the crevices in their trunks. Maybe these trees knew the Romans who built the columns she loves. Yellow daffodils nod and blossom between the chunky rock walls and terraces. She stoops to pick one for her mother.

The little girl can see her family house at the top of the hill, a two-story white stone building surrounded by fig and lemon trees, carob and pomegranate. To the side of the house is a sloping irrigated orchard of lush almond trees and grape vines. In the front wall of the house an ancient stone is embedded near the arched doorway. A stone stairway marches up the side to the second-floor apartment where her uncle's family lives. The donkey wanders nearby in the dry grasses, chewing contentedly.

Fatima's mother is squatting in front of the house with a cluster of aunts and village women just returned from sifting the grain after the men threshed the wheat with their heavy horse-drawn planks. Fatima loves to watch the villagers throwing the grain and straw in the air, creating great clouds of gold as the wind blows the straw to the side and heavy grain piles in the center.

Fatima can hear the women talking, her mother complaining. "Aye, with another baby coming, my back hurts from all the sitting on the ground. Aye, lifting my arms, shaking the sieve, blowing off the chaff. It's hard." Fatima sees bits of straw still stuck to the hem of her mother's long dress.

"Mama, I have a flower for you," Fatima calls.

"Binti, my daughter, where have you been?"

As Fatima runs towards the house, chickens and roosters scatter with a clatter of clucking and flapping. The doves coo gently in their cages and the sweet fragrance of roses drifts in the air. The women are squatting, grinding coffee beans with a stone mortar and pestle and making thick bitter coffee on a small kerosene stove. They serve the coffee in a round brass pot with a long spout like the beak of an exotic bird, as chickens peck hopefully around them.

Fatima can smell the bread baking in the stone taboon oven. The doughy smell mixes with the burning smoke and dried animal dung and branches used for fuel. Suddenly everyone goes silent as the rumble of motors can be heard in the distance. The women stand up and Fatima hides in the folds of her mother's dress.

"There, over there. Aye, may Allah protect us. What will they do to us this time?" Fatima's mother whispers. She squints her eyes and points deliberately. In the distance, at the base of the valley, they see the caravan of British jeeps and motorbikes with side carriers. They are roaring down the highway, leaving clouds raining dust and fear. Fatima starts crying and her mother rocks her, patting her head gently.

Fatima has heard the stories, how she was born during the second Arab Revolt. She has listened quietly, hidden in the front doorway of the house while her father smoked hookah with the other men. They squatted on flat cushions in the living room, or stretched out more comfortably in their loose, baggy pants and jackets. They drank coffee and talked of the fellahin in the countryside. These peasants took up arms and explosives to protest the British control over their lands and the sale of Arab lands to Yehudi, the Jewish settlers.

Fatima has heard her aunt whisper to her mother of what happened when Uncle Waleed was rounded up with other villagers. The men were made to sit in a wire cage in the hot, unrelenting sun for days until he died of thirst, with other men parched and gasping for breath. And then the British troops came into their village, invading people's homes, breaking their furniture, tearing up their Qurans.

Fatima has seen British soldiers only once, with their crisply curled mustaches, short tan pants, round hard hats, and strange sounding talk. They were standing in the market and looking at the village men with suspicion. Clutching her mother, she starts to shake uncontrollably; a sense of overwhelming dread washes over her like a giant wave in the field of wheat.

Her mother holds her tight, kissing her head, promising over and over, "Habibti, they cannot hurt you. I will protect you. I will keep you safe. Don't worry."

Chapter Eight

Then And Now

SITTI PAUSED FOR A MOMENT AND MOHAMMED LOOKED THROUGH the window at the concrete sidewalk outside and the rows of brick apartment buildings, the cars on his street, the honking, the traffic lights. He pictured the hamster at school and his pet iguana Iggy at home and all his old friends who had dogs and cats. He tried to picture his gray-haired grandmother as a young girl playing with goats and donkeys in some faraway place where the hills were terraced and dotted with contorted trees.

"Carrying water on your head? No showers?" Zaynab asked.

"On my head. No showers. Every drop of water was precious," said Sitti.

"Weird, that sounds like...ancient times," Mohammed said, looking curiously at his grandmother.

"What about the British soldiers? Did they come back?" asked Zaynab.

"The British? I'll tell you in a minute, but first, my village, my paradise." Mohammed noticed Sitti's face relax and her eyes reddened, wet with a film of tears and memory. "I loved the smell of the rose bushes and the cock-a-doodle-do of the roosters when the sun rose. My father kept doves, and in the evening, they would coo as the sun sank into the hills."

"Roosters? You had actual 5:00 in the morning, cock-a-doodle-do roosters?" Mohammed tilted his head and looked at her. "Real live doves? Sounds like you lived on some kind of farm."

"Well, habibi, it was more like a small village. We had chickens and fresh eggs every morning. And then there were our olive trees, some a thousand years old. They were like members of our family and many of them were given names, women's names."

"So that's why we eat so much olive oil?" said Zaynab. "It's the taste of home?"

"Ah yes. As a girl I used to hide in their curled branches, bending from the weight of the fruit." Sitti clapped her hands together. "Every year the whole family harvested the olives and crushed them into a clear, pure olive oil, the best in the village."

Mohammed stared out the window at a graceful maple tree in the tiny front yard. He loved to climb on its branches. *How old could it be? Fifty years max? What would he call it? Meredith the…magnificent maple? That sounded ridiculous. Could it ever live for a thousand years?*

"But what about the soldiers?"

His grandmother pulled them back into her story. "In the spring of 1948 there was a terrible war, a fight over the land of Palestine…"

"The British soldiers, with tanks and guns?" asked Mohammed.

"No, the British soldiers were gone by then. It was Israeli soldiers. I still remember it so clearly. I was ten years old, just a little older than you, Mohammed." Sitti pressed her palms to her ears and shook her head as if trying to shut out the sounds echoing in her brain.

"Soldiers were shooting at you, YOU?" asked Zaynab, shifting uneasily on the couch.

"Yes, shooting at your sitti."

Chapter Nine

Sitti's Story: Bayt Nattif – 1948

THE SLIGHTLY BITTER ONION AND GARLIC SMELLS OF MULOKHIYA soothe ten-year-old Fatima's nerves after the bombing two days earlier. She hands Mother a knife to cut up the chicken she has rubbed with lemon while her sisters, Layla and Dalia, chop cabbage and cauliflower.

"Bilal and Fadi, stop hiding behind the sacks of freekeh and barley. If they topple over we will have nothing to eat," Mother scolds.

Fatima carefully pours water out of a large jug to boil eggs on the kerosene stove for tomorrow's breakfast. The flame flickers as the water starts to bubble.

"Let me show you how to scoop out the eggplants," says Layla. "You need to learn to do it evenly so the stuffing won't fall out."

Fatima stares at the pyramid of small purple eggplants and a pile of freshly made flatbread and tightly rolled stuffed grape leaves. *I wanna cook like Mama. I can do this.* She sighs as the booming sounds of the bombing and thick black smoke return to her thoughts. She can still taste the nasty smell. Two days ago, the Israeli Air Force suddenly shelled the south side of the village and now she worries that no one knows what's next. Not even her parents.

She feels a shudder down her spine, her family was huddled together in the middle of the house, carefully staying away from the windows. Fatima put her hands over Bilal's ears and rocked him back and forth while Dalia cuddled the crying Fadi in a thick blanket. Mother grabbed two-year-old Darweesh as Yusef and Layla joined Father, dragging a table and blankets to make a protective barrier should something fall on their heads. The house stood, but still shook. Dishes clattered to the floor.

There were shards of broken glass everywhere. When Fatima cried, "Baba, I'm scared!" the younger children started screaming all over again.

As the roar of airplanes faded into the distance, Father said loudly, "The British are gone, but now the Haganah, the Jewish troops, are here." Then he stood very tall and looked directly at his children. "This is our land, the home of my father and his father before him and his father before that." He wiped his forehead with a dusty cloth. "Our family has been here for hundreds of years. No one can take this from us. May Allah protect us, praised be his name."

Fatima trembles. She had seen the tears in her father's eyes.

Fatima picks up an eggplant and thinks, *Baba says no one can take this away from us. No one. Who would feed the goats and the chickens and the doves and who would water the garden?* Bilal emerges from his hiding place and runs behind Fatima, grabbing her legs. "Stop. Can't you see I am cutting eggplants?" She glares at him. "You are so annoying."

As she reaches for another eggplant, the air abruptly crackles with a loud explosion followed by the rat-tat-tat of bullets in the distance.

Bilal screams and Fadi erupts into tears. Before anyone can speak, Father runs into the room and yells, "We have to leave now. The soldiers are coming."

Mother looks up, eyes wide with fear.

Another burst of gunfire crashes through the silence.

"Now!" bellows Father.

Mother grabs a basket and fills it with the flatbread and grape leaves, throws in the eggs, and tosses a blanket over the food as the three girls stare, unable to move.

Mother yells, "Layla you take Bilal. Dalia pick up Fadi. Fatima go find Darweesh." She opens a drawer, grabs her wedding jewelry, and stuffs it in her clothes. "Turn off the kerosene." They hear Father running upstairs to warn his brother's family, and soon there is a loud clunking of feet and the tap of grandpa's cane as everyone comes running down the stairs.

"Come on, Grandpa. Faster. Don't be slow," yells Fatima.

Father opens the carved wooden front door and looks in at his terrified family. He cautiously scans the hill. "Go," he commands. The family files out as if in a terrible dream, Grandpa's cheeks puffing with each step. Father locks the door, shoves a large iron key in his pocket, and starts to walk.

Fatima cries, "But Baba, what about the goats and my doll and…"

Father looks at her firmly, "Not now Fatima. Don't you hear the soldiers coming?"

They all jump and grab each other at the sound of another barrage of bullets, this time a little closer. Father's face softens and he says to Fatima, "Don't worry habibti. The Arab armies will protect us. We will be back in two weeks. I promise."

Fatima pleads, "But Baba, where are we going?"

Father looks at Mother. "East, we are walking east."

"East? Where's east?" Fatima questions. She looks up and sees a stream of people coming from all directions heading towards a dirt road that leads out of the village. She spots her aunts and uncles and countless cousins and people from the surrounding towns. She looks at their grim faces, the lumpy sacs thrown over their shoulders, the baskets and jugs on women's heads, the children carried on each hip, staring blankly or crying.

Fatima grips Darweesh's hand as he whines, "Too tight, too tight." The family joins the growing river of villagers. A shocked silence hangs in the air as their feet stir up a dusty cloud.

When they come up over a stony hill, Fatima gasps, "Soldiers!"

On each side of the road, a cluster of men and women, Israeli soldiers, guns pointed at the villagers, yell in Arabic, "Yalla, yalla. Faster, faster."

"Baba," she cries and turns to find her father in the dense crowd. She is relieved to see him right behind her, carrying Fadi. She turns back and puts her hand out to grab Darweesh again. She looks down. He is gone.

"Darweesh," she screams and suddenly Father and Mother are yelling his name, frantically searching the crowd. Fatima darts between people. "Darweesh, Darweesh? Have you seen my little brother? Brown trousers? White cap? No shoes? He's carrying a bag of marbles? He's little? Oh Darweesh."

The tears dribble down Fatima's cheeks when suddenly she spots him. "Mama, Baba, I see him. He's over there, on a rock by the side of the road. Sucking his thumb. He's staring at the soldiers."

Mother rushes over and scoops up her boy, hugging and patting him. "Habibi, habibi, we found you." She embraces him, shaking. "We have you. Fatima, do not let him go," she says sternly and lowers him to the ground.

Fatima stops crying, bends down, looks directly at her brother, and wraps her arms around him. She lifts him up, perches him on her hip, wipes her nose with her sleeve, and starts walking, staying close to her parents.

As the sun begins to disappear, Fatima says, "Mama, I'm tired. I'm hungry." She stares at her long shadow stretching in front of her. She imagines it is a strange ghost, leading her by her toes down this endless road. "Where is east?"

Mother looks at Father. He points to an orchard ahead. "We'll stop there," he says.

They join other families who are squatting by the road or under the olive trees, passing around whatever bits of food and water they had managed to grab, resting on blankets or the rocky soil. Fatima feels a growling tightness in her belly and painful blisters on her toes. Her sandals frayed miles ago and she smells the dust and sweat in her dress. She puts Darweesh down in front of her. "Don't move," she says loudly, and then plops herself on the dry grass, and puts out her hand. Mother hands them each a flatbread.

"Chew slowly. We do not have much," Mother says. "Aye, this baby is getting big already." She crouches on a flat stone and presses her hand into the small of her back.

Fatima leans against the trunk of an olive tree, tasting the familiar bread, watching her mother rubbing her aching muscles with the stars glowing beyond her. "Where are we going? When will we get there? When will we return home?" she asks, but before she can hear the answer, Fatima collapses into an exhausted sleep, dreaming of her donkey and the favorite goat she left behind.

WEDNESDAY

Chapter Ten

Tofu For Lunch

"**M**y friends," Ms. Santana announced at the beginning of independent reading on Wednesday, as she pushed her glasses up the bridge of her nose. "No talking. Please keep your hands to yourself and stay on task." Mohammed looked up at his classmates, some sitting on the carpet, others stretched out over a large pile of pillows. He remembered the story Sitti started telling him yesterday and found it hard to pay attention. *What happened to her? How long did she walk and to where? East? East of what?*

Okay brain, focus on school. He stared at the pillow kids. *They look like...a clump of seals...warming in the sun...at the aquarium.* That idea made him smile. He imagined the kids barking and slapping their sides.

"Ark ark," he giggled quietly, glad to have a new sound to play with.

Noah looked up. "Ark?" He shrugged. "Man, you okay?"

Other kids were hunched over books at their desks. Seth and Jacob wiggled. Jacob leaned over and poked Seth with a pencil.

"Ouch. Dude. What are you doing?"

Jacob flung his pencil and it landed with a bounce on Mohammed's desk. He looked up, startled.

"Gotcha, toad face. Diiiirrrt ball." Jacob dragged out the word dirt in a low menacing growl.

"Boys. Please," said Ms. Santana, her voice rising with frustration.

Mohammed's face flushed. He sunk lower into his chair and glanced over at Noah who was lost in his book. Mohammed bit his ragged nail and tried to focus. *I hate him, I hate him, I hate him.* He glanced up at a poster: READING, YOUR TICKET TO THE WORLD!

I need a ticket to get out of here. Right out of this town. I really need a ticket to…Boston… and Jacob? I'll give him a ticket to…Uranus. Right. He shoved Jacob's pencil onto the floor and turned to his open book, tried to focus, but the words wiggled on the page. The rolling pencil made a quiet clattering sound and came to a stop. He was distracted by the low rumble of voices in the classroom and his thoughts about Sitti.

He heard Noah tapping on the desk with his ruler. Noah looked up at Mohammed and they both nodded conspiratorially. Noah scribbled a message on a piece of paper, crunched it up, and tossed it to Mohammed.

WANNA PLAY AT RECESS?

Mohammed tucked his head down and stared at the message. He read it again and again. His mind drifted into a string of rhymes.

Don't be a dope, have hope…

He was searching for another rhyme when Ms. Santana's voice drilled into his consciousness.

"Now class, today we are going to talk about the words 'compare' and 'contrast.' Let's take two characters from the story we read yesterday and I am going to make a T-CHART." She drew a large "T" on the white board and wrote SAME on one side, DIFFERENT on the other. "Okay, think about the story. Can you tell me how the two characters are alike and how they are different?"

Amelia's hand shot up. "Amelia?"

"Well, like the cat is curious and the poodle is not, but they both have four legs." She announced with perky self-confidence.

"Yes, that's the idea. The two pets have different attitudes towards the family, one is curious, the other is not, and yet they are both four-legged animals. Anyone else?"

Mohammed watched as the list got longer and longer. The words "compare and contrast" rattled in his head. *I am like other fourth graders, two legs, two arms, one brain, SAME, but I am sooo DIFFERENT...but how? Ummm. Their grandmothers had...cats? My grandmother had a...goat. Oh great. Explain that to these...* He tried to think of the worst thing he had ever tasted...*these Brussels sprouts.*

He smiled, imagining his classmates as giant, kid-sized Brussel sprouts, with short little legs and arms sticking out from their enormous, green, lumpy, Brussel sprout bodies.

Brussel sprout, scream and shout, let me out... The words danced in his mind.

Suddenly he heard, "My friends, you may put away your books and get ready for recess."

There was a mad rush to the cubbies and the door. Emily grabbed her soccer ball. Jacob tripped over his untied high tops. Everyone laughed. Mohammed dragged his feet. Noah sidled up next to him at the end of the line and they shuffled outside. Noah gave him a friendly punch in the shoulder. Mohammed punched him back.

The sun was shining and the two boys started chasing each other. "You're fast," Noah laughed as he collapsed under a tree, breathing heavily. "You signed up for soccer?"

"Yup," answered Mohammed grinning.

"Well, I want you on my team, Mr. Mohammed Omar Mohammed."

He laughed again and Mohammed gave him a friendly shove and exclaimed, "Tofu for Lunch. That's what I'm calling you, Tofu." Soon the two boys were arm wrestling, grunting, laughing, their arms bulging and straining with effort.

Later that afternoon, Mohammed crumpled on the grass after zigzagging back and forth between the orange cones placed across the soccer field. Noah was just behind him, breathing heavily. They each took a swig from their water bottles.

Jacob was on the side lines arguing with Seth. "I didn't give you that Mini Slime, it's mine. Mine's green." He shoved Seth hard.

Seth swung back. "Nooooo, you moron. Yours is yellow."

Jacob sneered, "Noooo, dork face." He swiped at the container of Mini Slime, grabbed it, and started running just as Mohammed got up and was jogging back into practice. From the corner of his eye, he saw Jacob coming up out of nowhere.

Noah yelled, "Mo! Watch out."

Suddenly, Mohammed felt Jacob's foot behind him, then a swift whack at his heels and splat, he tumbled, flailed his arms, and fell forward, lying face first in the grass, a sharp little rock shoved into his cheek. "Nice footwork, klutz-ooo," Jacob sneered, juggling the Mini Slime in the air.

The cut on Mohammed's cheek oozed blood and he tasted the warm liquid dripping over his lip. Jacob was gone like a thunderbolt as the coach looked up and said, "Hey, you okay buddy? What happened?"

Mohammed rolled on his back and stared up at the blue sky. He touched his face, felt the warm, wet blood. *This place is like a war zone.* He blinked his eyes tightly and saw a gray black cloud piling up in the distance. His heart pounded and his cheek throbbed. War zones. *Are there blue skies or does the sky turn dark with black clouds when something bad is about to happen? School zones. War zones.* His mind drifted to Sitti. *Did someone hate her too? Did she get hurt?*

The coach came over, cleaned Mohammed's cheek with an alcohol swab, "Buddy, this is gonna burn," and pressed a Band-Aid over the bruise.

"Yoaw," groaned Mohammed, clenching his teeth.

"You okay big guy? Ready to play? Do you know the kid who did this?"

Mohammed was torn between rage and embarrassment. *Yeah, I tell him who did it and I am dead meat,* he thought. "No, I'm okay, I can play." He avoided the coach's eyes and scrambled to his feet, his cheek stinging.

The coach stood up and stared at him. "Let me know if you find out." Then he yelled, "Okay guys, good to go, no rest for the weary. Up, up, up."

Mohammed watched closely, his cheek aching, His eyes were focused on his feet and the ball. Noah looked at him and mouthed, "Are you okay? Jacob is a Jerk. Jerk."

Mohammed nodded a big yes. "Jerk. Jerk," he mouthed back, and jabbed his fist, thumb pointing upward.

As Mohammed warmed up, he concentrated more on the practice, getting faster, more confident, his feet sweeping back and forth, hugging the soccer ball. Noah followed after him, focusing on his own coordination and speed. As the coach added more footwork, the boys engaged in a friendly competition, Noah ran faster and faster, almost overtaking Mohammed. At the end of practice, they took turns kicking the ball into the net.

As the soccer ball tumbled forward, Noah yelled and pumped his fist, "Goal again. Victory. Yes."

After practice, Mohammed and Noah slumped under a tree at the edge of the field and each inhaled the rest of his water. "How's your war wound?" asked Noah.

"I think I'll live. Besides, the rest of the afternoon was... kind of fun," admitted Mohammed.

"Where did you play before?"

"Boston, been playing since I was five."

"Lucky you." Noah wiped the sweat off his forehead and looked at his new friend. "You told me at lunch about your Lego bridge, sounds cool. Can I check it out?"

Boy I would like that. But what if Sitti wants to feed him grape leaves or calls him habibi or tells him about some war? That would be too...I don't know...too embarrassing. He sat up straight and said, "Sure, but I'm...busy today. I need to talk to my grandma. I have to go home, but definitely, another day. I promise. Could you take this Band-Aid thing off?"

Chapter Eleven

A Very Long Story

AFTER SCHOOL AND SOCCER MOHAMMED UNLOCKED THE FRONT DOOR of his house with his shiny little key. He had a crusted purple bruise on his cheek, scrapes on his palms, and a new bounce in his step. *Maybe I will live through fourth grade after all, just maybe. I have to...cope, oh that's the word I was looking for. Rhymes with hope. Cope.*

He saw Zaynab curled up on the couch, chatting on her phone. "Monica, I miss you Moca Bean. This move has been sooo tough. I need to find a friend here, you know, like you Bean."

"No. You're right. No, you are the queen of friends. But listen to this." Zaynab stretched out one leg and picked at a loose thread on her jeans.

Mohammed quietly put his backpack down on the floor and stood in the doorway. *Stand tall. Be a fly on the wall.*

"Thanks for the hugs, Bean, but listen up. This idiot boy walks over to me, points to my hijab and says, 'Why are you wearing that? Do you wear it in bed? In the shower? What color is your hair? Do you even have hair?'"

"Right, can you believe that? I didn't know if I should laugh or cry." She twirled a thick curl of hair around her finger. "Or try to explain stuff about Islam to him." She stopped for a moment. "I wanted to slap his face."

Mohammed listened intently to his sister. He shook his head and slowed his breath to near silence. That would be a good feeling, shoving Jacob as hard as he could. In the face. A satisfying punch. Bam.

"And then one of his buddies started taunting me with, 'Does your dad wear a turban? TUR-BANNNN!' So dumb." She sat up straight and stretched out her other leg, pushing herself forcefully back into the pillows. "By that point I just yelled, 'Wrong religion, you jerk.'"

"You're right; I shouldn't have lost my temper. But it is so hard, all that Muslim compassion stuff. I feel like I am the little Muslim ambassador at my school, like if I screw up it will be even tougher for my sisters and brother."

"Right! Or any other Muslim kid who happens to stumble into this hell."

That would be me. Mohammed shifted uneasily in the doorway.

"Yeah, on top of that, every time I raise my hand in math, this one girl just glares at me, like, girls don't do math. It's so stupid." She caught another curl and pulled it straight.

"And then this boy said, 'I'm sooo surprised you're sooo good in math. When did you learn English?' I wanted to scream, I was born here you idiot. When did you learn English?"

"Yeah I know. I didn't say it, but it was so tempting."

There was a pause. "Really, and if I am already on the weird not-really-a-true-blue-American list, just imagine when Ramadan comes and I'm fasting from dawn to dusk and all the kids are chomping down lunch in the cafeteria. If I leave, everyone knows I'm gone and I miss all the good gossip and just feel like more of an outsider. So, do I just sit there and watch the cows chewing their cuds?"

"No Moca Bean, there is no mooing in the cafeteria, but I get your drift. Plus, when the fasting begins I get so sleepy-hungry-thirsty in the afternoon."

Mohammed felt so hungry when he tried to fast, even just skipping a meal here and there. *I am so glad I am too young to fast all day.*

"It's gonna be…lonely." Zaynab stared across the living room at the packed boxes of books and took a deep breath.

"Well yeah, I could hang in the library, but if there are exams or track meets. It's extra hard. Hard to concentrate. Hard to run. I just don't want to mention anything to the coaches."

"I know you think I should, but I'm afraid they won't let me play." She raised one eyebrow and nodded.

"Right, and swim team tryouts start next week too."

Mohammed slowly sank onto a taped up box of books by the doorway. He bit his fingernail.

Another long pause. Zaynab nodded and picked up her scarf folded over the end of the couch, and draped it over her knees.

"You know my butterfly is even better than my freestyle. But I'm not talking strokes here…"

Mohammed coughed suddenly and Zaynab's head whipped towards the door.

"Oh god, what happened to my brother? Gotta go. Love you Bean."

Mohammed stood up and grabbed his book bag.

"Baby brother? Your face?"

"Zaynab, it's nothing. NOTHING."

"I don't believe you. Did that jerk boy whack you in the face?"

"None of your business."

Mohammed strode toward the kitchen and called to his grandmother. "Sitti, can we talk now?"

"Mohammed, look how grimy you are." Sitti gasped, "Oh my gracious, what happened to you? Did someone hit you?"

Mohammed replied, "It's nothing, forget it."

She gave him a funny look. "Doesn't look like nothing to me."

Zaynab chimed in from the other room. "It's definitely not nothing, trust me."

"Mohammed, tell me," Sitti said firmly.

Mohammed shrugged and sighed, bouncing slowly on the balls of his feet, "Okay, well…that dufus Jacob, he pushed me during soccer practice and I fell on my face, I think I hit a rock. But I had fun with Noah. I think we're like friends."

Sitti nodded her head. "I know what that feels like, getting hit in the face."

"You do?"

"It happened when we left the village, on the long walk east. It was a soldier. We weren't moving fast enough. I was hungry, really wanted to pick some apricots. I was only ten."

Zaynab peaked into the kitchen. "He hit you?"

"He hit me with the end of his rifle."

"Sitti, you have to tell us what happened. Everything. I mean, I could barely think about school all day." Mohammed looked at her, eyebrows raised.

"Okay. Let's go sit in the living room. It's a long story."

"I'm gonna listen too," Zaynab announced and flounced dramatically to the end of the couch.

Sitti smiled as they curled up on the soft cushions. Zaynab moved further away. Mohammed noticed a faint scar on Sitti's left cheek. *Was that it?* And what was the shiny scar covering the back of her hand?

"Baby brother, I need my space here and don't touch my phone."

"Don't touch my phone," taunted Mohammed mimicking Zaynab. He wiggled towards his grandmother and glared at his sister.

"Children, please. Just let it go. There are more important battles to fight."

Sitti's voice got that dreamy, faraway sound.

"When we fled, after the attack by the soldiers, we hid in a cave for months. By the end of the war, the area we were in was controlled by the Jordanians.

"Wait," Zaynab said. "I thought you were attacked by Israeli soldiers, I mean in Palestine which the…British had controlled?"

"The British pulled out before the war. When the war started, the Arab League joined forces to oppose the creation of Israel, on our land.

"Okay, so…?"

"So…at the end of the war, the Jordanians controlled the area where we were hiding. In a cave."

"A cave? Like with bats?" asked Mohammed.

"Such misery." Sitti stopped for a minute.

"Finally, the United Nations built us a small cement house with two rooms for my mother and father, seven children, and my grandparents. Can you imagine?"

Chapter Twelve

Sitti's Story: The Cave – 1949

NEXT TO THE ROUGH GRAY STONE, FATIMA SITS OUTSIDE the entrance to the cave, warming herself near a small fire pit, eating a bowl of watery lentils. "If we ever get out of this, I will never eat lentils again," she says to her grandfather. She rubs the aching scar on the side of her left cheek and remembers the sharp pain of the rifle butt, the angry soldier voice, her footsteps running, running across a field, hands clutching the ripe apricots she had gathered.

Shivering in her thin, faded dress, she feels the damp cool air on her skin and huddles up against him. "Why is it taking so long?" she asks.

She picks up the metal pots piled near the pit and taps her finger along the edge, singing. "Baby, baby, how long, how long." Her old donkey had a baby before they fled the village.

One day she lay down on her side, panting and pushing until the shaky, wet calf was born. "What's happening to mama?" she asks her grandfather.

Suddenly they hear a wailing from inside the darkness. As she peeks into the cave her grandfather pulls her away. But she has seen everything. Her grandmother kneeling over her mother. Her mother lying on blankets on the floor. Her aunt stroking her forehead. Blood was everywhere.

Grandfather wraps her up in his arms as she starts to cry. "Let's go, habibti, let's walk. You should not see this." Then they both stop, waiting for the sounds of the newborn.

There is nothing but brutal silence. Suddenly her mother lets out a deep moaning shriek. "Noooo."

Chapter Thirteen

Sitti's Story: Aida Refugee Camp, Bethlehem - 1950

TWELVE-YEAR-OLD FATIMA REACHES FOR THE RAGGED WET shirts and pants in the bucket and hangs them to dry on the ropes that support her family's drab, gray tent. She stretches her back and squints against the sun, staring at the rows of tents in every direction. *I wonder what happened to my favorite goats back in the village. I miss them so.*

She can hear the laundry flapping quietly, threadbare white tee shirts and patterned skirts and shirts draped over ropes, between tents, like faded flags from some long-lost nation. She wrinkles her nose as the fetid smell of open sewage drifts up from the nearby latrine.

Fatima remembers the warm feel of the sun setting over the village fields, the freshness in the air, but before she can get lost in her thoughts, she feels a growl from her empty stomach. She sees Yusef winding his way between the tents, a scrum of flies buzzing around his head. His hair is shaved from a recent bout of lice. "Yusef, did the UN trucks bring the flour yet?"

"I have a sack of lentils, no flour. The other sac is rice, alhamdulillah, praise Allah," he responds, shifting the heavy burlap bags on his shoulders. He blinks his eyes, irritated by the crusting and redness that has bothered him for weeks. He tries to wipe his eyelids with his sleeve.

Fatima sighs, "Lentils again."

Her father lights a cigarette and squats next to Grandfather, the dark mouth of the tent opening behind them. A sac of sugar leans against the tent flap, and a can of vegetable oil piled against tins of egg powder catches the glint of the sun. "Aye, we are low on flour, how will we feed the children? I tell you, there is no future here. Does the world even know of our suffering? Even the Jordanians do nothing. Are they blind?"

Fatima bends down to hug her father. "Baba, we won't be here forever. The UN says it is only temporary. You said we will go back home soon. Don't be sad."

"Ah, my Fatima," her father smiles. "You always lift my spirits. But habibti, what do I say to your six brothers and sisters? We are all hungry. And Grandfather too. And there is no work here. May Allah protect your dead baby sister; at least she is not suffering."

A spasm of coughing makes him stop talking. Fatima stares at the thick blood-stained phlegm in his hand. She thinks about the DDT dust the authorities sprayed on everyone when they entered the camp last year. *Did that make him sick? Maybe he's coughing from misery.*

Mother comes walking up the path carrying two boxes of condensed milk and five tins of sardines, "Product of Norway" stamped on each can. "There was so much pushing and shoving to get to the food handouts today. There were crates of sardines, but too many hungry mouths to feed.

"Was there another delivery?" Father asks.

"I ran when I heard the UNRWA trucks rumbling in, but still, there is never enough. So many people arguing and grabbing. So many desperate families, starving kids." She shakes her head and clucks her tongue. Fatima can see the weary disappointment in her mother's eyes.

A crowd of barefoot children chasing a tattered ball runs in front of Mother, nearly knocking her over. She hears their laughter and says, "At least the children still find happiness." Fatima looks at the pack of children and wishes she could run after that ball. *I have to help Mama. I'm twelve, I'm no longer a child.*

"Fatima, did you hear there is going to be a football game and Yusef and Bilal are on two of the teams? They will play in the fields that are owned by the Armenian Church behind the camp, across from the olive groves."

Grandfather stares at Mother, silently puffing his cigarette, his white keffeyeh wrapped loosely around his neck, his cheeks sunken and creased. His mouth is etched in a permanent, bitter frown. Fatima gives him a hug, inhaling the smell of his unwashed body, whiffs of sweat, tobacco, and cardamom, but he barely responds. She sees the tears in his eyes and lifts his darkly wrinkled hand in hers. "Grandfather, it will be better, insha'allah, God willing. At night, there are still stars in the sky. That's what you always told me. Look at the stars and they will light the way home." She snuggles her face into his white beard. "I love you Grandfather."

He hugs Fatima just as a gust of wind blows sand into the tent. She sees a delicate coat of white powder covering the pile of thin mattresses and blankets. "Grandfather, at least we are not living in that awful cave anymore. It is drier here and the floor is not rough stones.

"Aye."

"That was no place for us to live or for Mama to have her baby. It was too cold and Mama was so sick."

Grandfather nods and Fatima leans over and kisses him, his skin like bristly leather. She plops herself next to his legs. "Tell me the stories of our village. Again, Grandfather, again," Fatima says. "Fill me with your stories."

He looks at her with distant, watery eyes and inhales a long breath on his cigarette. As he exhales slowly, Fatima watches the gray smoke curl above his head. "Aye, Fatima. In Nattif, we had a beautiful house and olive trees and almonds. You remember?"

Fatima smiles. She wishes she could live on stories rather than food.

"It was like heaven. Your grandmother, she made maqluba and we ate lamb and...Remember the wheat fields and the sweet smell of the wind coming up from the valley? And your uncle Waleed was still alive, now he could tell stories...." His voice drifts off as he floats into his memories. His cigarette hangs between his lips, quivering slightly, and he closes his eyes, shaking his head.

Fatima waits and watches. She squeezes his arm and sees his forehead furrowing into a deep frown. "Grandfather, you can tell me more later. Look, there's Dalia and Layla." Her two older sisters walk slowly between the tents and ropes carrying water jugs on their heads. They avoid families squatting around open fires and children playing in the sand. The children are making piles of small round stones, rolling them into empty cans with a satisfying "ploink."

"I heard another convoy of UNRWA trucks is coming soon, today," says Dalia.

Fatima takes off running towards the food distribution center just as the canvas covered UNRWA trucks rumble in. She watches as men start unloading large bags of flour. She cannot read, but she recognizes the label: two hands clasped with stars above and stripes below and the letters U, S, and A. Yusef taught her the letters. *Where is this U.S.A. and why do they give us flour?*

Mother comes behind her carrying a sack for her flour ration as one large bag is ripped open and a man from the camp takes out a large metal scoop. Mother and Fatima get in line together, crowded by the gathering refugees as word spreads through the camp that the truck has arrived. Fatima hugs her mother and realizes she is tall enough to stare into her mother's eyes. She recognizes her exhausted look and hears the chatter of ragged children, their feet kicking up sand as they run.

Mother says, "After we get the flour, we will go to that market at the front of the camp and try to buy some onions and maybe even oranges. I still have a little jewelry left we can trade for food."

"And then what mama?" Fatima says. "What happens when your jewelry is gone?" Fatima burrows her bare toes into the sand, digging little rows that remind her of plowing in the spring. "I said, then what mama?" she insists, feeling more desperate. "When there is no money left, then what happens to us?"

Chapter Fourteen

Gold Coins And Hungry Kids

SITTI STOPPED FOR A MOMENT AND INHALED DEEPLY. "Finally, we moved to that tiny cement house built by the UN. With the public toilet down the alley. Seven kids and my parents and grandparents.

"Wait, that's ten people in two rooms?" Mohammed asked.

Sitti nodded. "I can still remember the arguments. In those two little rooms we were always on top of each other."

Mohammed looked at Zaynab, his eyes wide, eyebrows arched sharply upward. He shared a room with his sisters. Marwa was very neat but Dima just dropped her stuff anywhere, and Zaynab was always telling them, "Will you shut up? Can't you see, I'm trying to study here?" They fought over small things like picking up dirty clothes on the floor or sharing the space on the desk or Marwa's stinky sneakers. But five more brothers and sisters and maybe his grandparents all in the same room? *Yikes.*

"Where did you sleep? Did your grandparents…like snore or anything?" he asked.

"We put thin mattresses on the floor and all slept curled up against each other…like a pile of my stuffed grape leaves." Sitti laughed. She stopped for a moment, remembering the cramped, comforting closeness of all those related bodies, the smells of sweat and spice.

"Of course, everyone snored…and burped and coughed at night."

And I bet they farted. Mohammed's lips curled into a tiny smile. The thought of his sitti farting. He chuckled quietly.

"And then…slowly, slowly, I grew up." She slapped her hands on her legs.

"Come into my room. I have something to show you." She grabbed Mohammed's hand. Zaynab unfolded her long legs and followed.

They walked into Sitti's bedroom. She bent over and opened the bottom drawer of her dresser. "See what you can find this time." Under the collection of folded scarves, Mohammed felt a small tattered bag of gold coins. He ran his fingers over five gold bracelets worn with age. He touched a faded photograph of a cement house and a young woman.

"Is that real gold?" asked Zaynab.

"Yes."

"Is that you?" Mohammed asked. The young woman was wearing a cloth hat ringed by coins, mostly silver, some gold, and a long, embroidered dress.

"Ah, I was once considered a beautiful girl. When I was sixteen I got married. Yes, that young woman in the photo is me."

Zaynab looked at her grandmother. "You were the same age as me? I can't imagine getting married, I mean at sixteen."

"You sure don't have any gold jewelry," snickered Mohammed. He knew Zaynab was already talking about going to college, becoming an engineer. *Marriage, babies. Yuck, no way. She doesn't even know how to cook. What would she eat?*

"Well it's not happening any time soon, trust me baby brother." Zaynab looked seriously at her grandmother. "Sitti, did you love him?"

"Ah, this was another time. We didn't talk about love, but we grew into love, as the years went by, like two flowers in the same pot. It's a different rhythm than now."

"Really?" Zaynab stared at Sitti, bending her head sideways like a big question mark.

"As was the tradition, your sedo, your grandpa, he and I, we lived upstairs from his parents. We didn't have much, but the custom then was to give the bride gold coins and jewelry, and then when times were hard, we sold the gold. You see the hat?"

Mohammed stared at the photo. "Yup." She pointed at the coins sewed in rows on the cloth.

"Well, the silver coins replaced the gold coins we used when we were hungry. Sometimes Sedo didn't have work and sometimes he just didn't get paid."

Mohammed asked, "Were *you* hungry?"

Sitti looked down at her lap, rubbing her fingers worriedly, and said, "Yes, even my children. I remember."

"Your children?" Mohammed stared at Sitti with her difficult long-ago life, with that kind of desperate hunger. He couldn't even see skipping breakfast, unless he was really nervous or trying a mini fast for Ramadan. He looked at Sitti's face, a mix of pleasure and sadness in her moist eyes. A wave of guilt swept over him when he thought of Noah trashing his lunch and all that wasted food.

Mohammed wiggled off the couch, leaned over his grandmother, and gave her a long hug. Sitti cleared her throat as if trying to squelch her sadness before it escaped.

Chapter Fifteen

Aida Refugee Camp, Bethlehem – 1961

TWENTY-THREE-YEAR-OLD FATIMA TAKES THE HAND OF four-year-old Allam and perches one-year-old Seema on her hip, her belly already bulging with the next baby. Her older sister Dalia hurries next to her with her son and daughter trailing behind. The women kiss on each cheek, back and forth three times. "Where's Layla?" asks Dalia.

"With this pregnancy she's always late getting kids to school. Life is hard with her three older kids in the morning shift and the twins in the afternoon classes. She is so tired, with her legs so swollen," replies Fatima, shaking her head.

"Those seven kids, that will make you tired," says Dalia.

"And she gets so little help from her mother-in-law," adds Fatima.

"I worry with the last baby still so young and so weak. And look at her husband, that Saeb. Not to criticize, but he wants a big family. Taking care of the children? That's another story," says Dalia, shaking her head.

"Of course, his sisters are helpful, but they have families of their own," replies Fatima. "Right, and she always complains about Saeb's snoring, how can she get any sleep in that house?" says Dalia.

"I know," says Fatima, "Mohammed groans in his sleep a lot, but nothing compared to his mother. What a groaner that woman is. You know, sleep or no sleep, my Mohammed is a good husband."

"You are very lucky."

"But we still don't have enough to eat and never enough money."

"Does anyone have enough money here? We are all living like beggars," adds Dalia, her voice angry. A flock of birds startles and flies up to a rooftop.

Fatima shakes her head. "Look, I'm married for seven years, and I can't believe we are still in this awful place, waiting and waiting for something to change."

"Like the sardines in those cans from Norway," says Dalia.

Fatima nods, grinds her teeth, and wrinkles her brow with frustration. She gives Seema a gentle hug. "When the UN started building those tiny concrete houses, one room for the whole family, I wondered, will they ever let us go home? Is this what we deserve? Aye, the birds have more freedom than we do."

Dalia nods bitterly, "It doesn't look like they will ever let us go home, sister. And while we are stuck here, do they provide electricity? Water? No. It's like they don't think we are human."

Her son jumps up and down, tossing a smooth rock back and forth into a tin can, making a sharp pinging sound. "Put that down," Dalia barks and swats his head abruptly.

"But mama." His eyes well with tears.

"Don't bother me now. Aye, Fatima. We have lived in this refugee camp for so many years the days blend together. I have no patience with the children. The winter nights are too cold, the summers too hot."

"And I can't stand the stinky smells," adds Fatima, stepping over a thin river of sewage. "Kids, look out."

"Remember the clear water I used to carry from that spring in Nattif?" asks Dalia.

"I said put that down now" she snaps. Her son drops the can with a thump and pouts, dragging his feet in the sand. He turns around and shoves his sister really hard.

"Stop. Mama, Shadi hit me," she cries.

"If I hear one more thing out of the two of you…."

Fatima responds, "Oh, don't be harsh Dalia. They're kids. They're so skinny, always hungry, bored. And the lice. You know, the worst thing for me is the sick children…and the hunger of course. Oh, I can't bear when my children are hungry."

"And all the diarrhea only makes it worse," Dalia nods. "Their poor little bottoms."

Layla comes rushing, puffing up the packed sandy path with her seven-year-old twins skipping in front of her. She catches her breath. "Sisters. Sorry I am late. The line at the latrine was sooo long and with this pregnancy, I am peeing all the time."

Both sisters laugh and chime in, "That's for sure."

The cousins start running around their three mothers, poking each other and laughing. Dalia snaps again and grabs her daughter's hand. "Enough. Kids. Just walk. No jumping."

The mothers and children slowly make their way between rows of white, concrete block structures, small square buildings, each with a tiny window and a door.

"At least these one room houses are better than those awful tents," says Layla.

An old neighbor coughs loudly and cackles, "Um Omar, As-salaam 'alaykum." He raises his hand in greeting. A young woman squats near him in a long, embroidered dress, cooking flatbreads draped over a large blackened pot on an open fire, her sleeves loose around her bony wrists.

"Stay away from the flames," Layla warns the children.

Suddenly, the young woman's sleeve catches fire. She screams, waving her arm frantically, trying to put out the flames. Fatima drops Seema and rushes to help, swatting the blaze with the back of her hand as the woman cries and wriggles in pain. Someone throws a pot of water on both of them, smoke and the smell of burnt skin and cloth wafts in the air. The children stand, mouths open, transfixed. Layla and Dalia hide the eyes of the little ones, "Don't watch baba, don't watch."

Fatima clutches her wrist around her charred sleeve as the skin on the back of her hand reddens and a cluster of blisters explode. She moans and sways back and forth. The other woman squats in the sand, rocking and crying. An old woman runs towards Fatima and rubs buttery samneh gently onto her burn while another woman approaches, carrying a jug of olive oil. "You poor girls, rub this on your skin. Olive oil, it's good for burns." An older man shuffles towards both of them with clean rags to wrap their injuries.

One neighbor grabs the burned flatbread off the blackened pot; others crouch around the gathered crowd, holding their coffee, cigarettes hanging loosely from the lips of the men talking in low voices as the smoke drifts around their heads.

"I hope the burns aren't too bad."

"These fires, so dangerous with all these kids running around."

"Lucky we caught it quickly."

"Of course we caught it, nothing happens in private here. The camp is so crowded."

The young woman in the burned, embroidered dress catches Fatima's eye. "Thank you Um Omar. You really saved my life, or at least my arm." They stare at each as if bound together by their burning skin and mutual catastrophe.

Fatima steels herself as she looks at the wide-eyed children. She can't control the flood of sorrow and rage welling inside or the searing pain in her hand. She wants it all to stop, the throbbing, the bitter life in the camp, the lice, the parasites, the moments of resignation and hopelessness in her children's faces. She desperately wants a better life for them, better than the one she has been dealt. There is no space in this crowded camp for weakness.

Fatima hugs Seema with her good hand. "I'm okay. Don't be afraid." She straightens up and bites her lip, her face tightening. "We mustn't be late for Omar." She nods towards the injured woman and her father. "So sorry this happened." They nod back, the woman quietly weeping, holding her arm like a sling. "Insha'allah, we will heal quickly." Fatima's jaw hardens, her stoicism crushing the torrent of fury and hurt surging through her, like an unexploded bomb left in the dirt by a soldier, just waiting to erupt.

Fatima nods goodbye. She stops for a moment to catch her breath. "I can't believe it…So much happened. So fast. There is pain everywhere we turn and now this." She hoists Seema onto her hip with her uninjured hand. She clenches her jaw. "We can't let it stop us."

Her sisters hug her gently.

"Sister, this camp has so many dangers, but you seem so strong."

"Dalia, I am blessed with children and a good husband and a mother-in-law with energy to help with the cooking. I cannot fail them. Let's walk."

Dalia herds the children along. "But sister, there is always someone in the family who can drive you crazy."

Fatima smiles with a whisper of an impish grin, "Nothing is perfect. Mohammed's father…way too strict with Omar."

Layla nods in agreement, "Sister, he is impatient with everybody. His bitterness poisons even his coffee."

Fatima laughs resentfully. "How long can we survive this way?" Seema pulls at the embroidery on her mama's sleeve. "Oh, you poor darling," Fatima says, kissing her head.

"Mama? Mama? I wanna see Omar. I wanna go." Allam tugs on her dress. Fatima looks down at her little boy and smiles. She ruffles his hair cautiously with her exposed fingers as the odor of charred cloth clings to her body. They walk past an old woman rocking back and forth, sitting in a doorway. Her face is creased and brown from the sun.

Dalia says, "So many young children with no place to play and their parents and grandparents just watching and waiting." They hear yelling, a loud slap, and a child crying. From another doorway comes a noisy giggle as two children tickle each other.

Fatima corrals Allam with her wrapped up hand. "I can't hold your hand habibi, stay close. Let's go meet Omar. Come along little ones. Let's walk a bit faster. Who can gallop like… like…a racing camel?"

Fatima looks at her sisters as they pick up their pace. "I am so tired now, and this injury. How will I feed this next baby? But what choice do we have?"

Dalia looks at her gently and says, "But you always have dreams. You are so fierce."

Fatima nods, "Oh yes, I have dreams and I have strength, insha'allah." She shakes her head defiantly, looking up at the horizon, and marches forward with the parade of jumping children.

Layla complains, "I can't keep up with you." They slow down. "Did you hear the rumor about my neighbor's daughter and the boy who lives near the market?"

Dalia retorts, "All the gossip bothers me, everyone knows everybody's business."

Layla continues, "So much yakking…Sometimes I feel I can't even breathe."

"Privacy? What's that? You can't even fart in private," Fatima laughs bitterly. "My mother-in-law knows everything. What with one room bursting with clothing, mattresses, pots, and sacks of flour and sugar."

"And your growing family and your husband's parents and four of their unmarried children in that tiny space," adds Dalia.

Fatima smiles. The small vegetable garden she planted behind her house gives her hope, it has no walls and no roof. Just wind, rain, and sky.

"We are all crowded together like a herd of goats."

"All bleating at each other," says Dalia.

"And butting each other," Layla laughs.

"Seriously Layla, my garden is my solace." She turns her head towards her little girl, "We will soon have tomatoes and squash, my little cucumber," she says to Seema, tickling her belly.

As Seema giggles, sticks her thumb in her mouth, and shakes her thick black hair back and forth, Fatima inhales the smells of bread baking, coffee boiling, and the sour sweat of unwashed children. She hears the squeals and laughter of kids running in the sand.

"Watch out. Slow down," chastises Dalia.

Fatima stops for a moment. "Do you remember the fields of barley, the harvest smells, and my favorite donkey with the big dark eyes?" She looks at her sister, Layla. "These poor children, all they know is the camp. But what do we know anymore?"

"That's right," answers Layla. "All we have are memories and hope."

"And the power in my heart to survive, if only for my children," adds Fatima. She hugs Seema and sweeps away her thick hair from her eyes. "Fierce like a tiger," she growls, and nuzzles her baby girl. Seema laughs.

Layla nods, "You are so good with your children. You are really sweet, like honey and rose water."

"Oh, would I like a taste of that," responds Fatima. She listens to the distant clatter and chatter from an open market on the edge of the camp. "I don't even know if I have enough money to buy a chicken."

Dalia says, "You must bargain harder, remind that butcher that the children are hungry. Show him your bandaged hand. Soften up his heart of stone. And remember, he'll overcharge if you are not careful."

The kids run up to a goat that wanders across their path, bleating, "Baaa, baaa." "Ha Ha, his beard looks like Grandfather's," laughs Shadi.

"His teeth too," says his cousin.

"That's not nice. Get over here," says Dalia. The children grab each other's hands and follow their mothers around a long line of people waiting to use the public latrine.

"Aye, there is so much waiting here," Fatima says, turning to Allam.

"I see the school," shouts Allam excitedly, pointing to a very large gray tent with rows of thick white tent stakes pounded into the sand. Allam and his cousins run up to the opened flaps and stare into the big school room. The sunshine streams in through the gaps where the flaps are tied up around the edges. Fatima can see the fifty children squeezed together under the tent.

Soon the cousins spot their brothers and sister. Allam finds his brother, Omar. Omar nods and squirms, crowded beside his three cousins at a rough wooden desk. He bends down from his seat and hands a booklet to one of the many children sitting in the aisles on the sand. Two other children scramble for the book, shoving each other.

"It's my turn," one complains.

"No, it's mine," the other answers, grabbing at the paper.

"Mine," says the first child.

Ten hands shoot up as Mohammed, the teacher, holds up two fingers on one hand and five fingers on the other. "There's Baba," grins Allam, looking back as his mother slowly approaches the tent, breathing heavily from her pregnancy, leaning on Dalia, twisting her injured hand back and forth.

"Shhh, don't talk too loudly, Allam. School is not quite over for today." Fatima puts her arm around her son and says, "Habibi, someday you will learn to read. You will learn history and mathematics."

She sighs. "I only wish I could read, but my children, you will all go to school. And maybe you will be a teacher like your papa, or a nurse …or maybe an engineer and then you will build your mama a stone house, right next to Grandfather's."

"I will build you a real house," Allam says impishly. "You'll see. With lots of rooms." Fatima gives him an affectionate hug and kisses his cheek.

"And I'll help too," chimes in one of his cousins. "I'm very strong…and smart too."

Mohammed waves to Fatima as he dismisses the school children. The students file out of the school tent, holding hands or wrapping their arms around each other's shoulders. Fadi, Ghada, and Amr come running up to Layla. "Mama, Mama," Amr yells and encircles his ten-year-old arms around her waist.

Mohammed walks over to his wife and takes a small sack of bread and a boiled egg from her. "What happened to your hand?"

Fatima shakes her head, "Just a little burn. Don't worry."

"Of course I worry," his eyes stare intently. "You sure?"

She nods dismissively, biting her lip as her hand throbs.

"Be careful habibti. We will talk more later. The second shift will be starting soon. I am doing my best with so little, these children desperately need to learn. I have no time to breathe"

"I understand," says Fatima nodding.

"I could use more pencils and of course, notebooks." Fatima agrees as more children come streaming in from all directions towards the school.

Fatima says, "You know, I always say education is everything. At least no one can take that away. And you are giving them that great treasure."

"Not even the Israelis," Dalia adds with a wave of bitterness. "First they steal our land, then they expel us, but they cannot steal our minds."

Mohammed shakes his head in agreement. Fatima can see a shadow of resentment and worry cross his face. He walks back into the tent, picking up a pile of creased notebooks on one of the desks.

Omar runs to his mother. "I got all the math problems right," he crows and dances around in the sand. "And we are making a play about Palestine. I want to tell about our village, how there was bombing and we were thrown out and walked for days. You've told me all the stories. I want to play Grandfather," he says. "I will show everyone the big iron key to the old house."

Ghada adds, "I want to tell how we will return to our olive trees, how our family's olive oil was the best in the village."

"And remember the almonds and the lemon trees." Fatima smiles and kisses Seema on her cheek. She shifts the child on her hip and says, "I still dream of my house and the wheat fields. Someday, we will go back. Hopefully soon, insha'allah. Never forget, my little dreamers."

She gestures towards Allam and Omar, "Come. We need to get back to the camp. I have a checkup at the clinic. Maybe they can look at the burn too. Sisters, I will see you later."

They start walking down a sandy path, passing a small bakery and a butcher shop with a slaughtered sheep. The carcass hangs from a large hook and flies buzz and dive bomb. Fatima shoos the flies away from Seema's head as she points to the raw meat.

Allam says, "Mama, can you buy that?"

Fatima shakes her head no. "I wish, someday. Someday when we have so many dinars, we won't know what to do." Her laughter turns sour.

Omar stops, "You okay Mama?"

"Of course, your mama is always okay, more than okay. I've got you, my dearest." A shoemaker hammers on a sole, working at his bench in the sun and a few chickens scatter as they walk. Soon they are heading towards another large tent where lines of women and children cluster and wait, passing the UNRWA CLINIC sign.

"Mama, more waiting? So many people ahead of us. I wanna play," whines Omar. "I don't want a shot today, pleeease."

Fatima replies, "No shots for you, but yes, of course more waiting. There is always more waiting." She pats her belly as the baby inside squirms and kicks. "Ah little one, I have dreams for you too. You will go to school, maybe you will be a doctor and take care of your old mother, and someday we will all return to our village. I believe it will happen. All in good time, but not soon enough."

THURSDAY

Chapter Sixteen

Confusalated

O N Thursday, Mohammed watched Ms. Santana write on the white board. She turned to the class and said, "Today we are going to start a research project about who we are and where we come from."

Several of the boys groaned, and Jacob snorted, "I'm from Mars."

There was a burst of giggles interrupted by Ms. Santana, "Boys, please. This is a serious topic. Everyone has family. Some families have lived here for a long time, some have arrived recently. People come from different places in the world, from different cultures, for different reasons."

Mohammed squirmed uncomfortably in his chair. *Like me.*

"Native Americans are thought to have traveled from Asia more than 15,000 years ago," she continued. "And like I said, other folks may have arrived last week.

"So, people come from different countries, different continents, and now we are all living here. Help me, friends. Can anyone name a country their family comes from?"

Three hands shot up. "Emily?"

"My family is from England and Ireland, but my grandmother says I am kind of a mutt."

"Well the expression 'mutt' means you have different ancestors from different parts of the world and you are a blend of all of them. Which I think makes you really unique. Amelia?"

"My family is from Germany, but I was named after Amelia Earhart because my dad was a pilot."

"Okay. Seth?"

"My family is from somewhere in Africa, but 'cause of slavery, we don't know where exactly. And my dad says my blue eyes mean I have white ancestors too, maybe from England."

"Yes, the fact that so many people were enslaved and were forced here, makes this whole subject much more challenging. So many difficult unknowns. So much suffering. And of course, most everyone has a mix of different ancestors. But friends, you can see that looking at just three people, we have families from over four different countries."

Jacob made a loud clunking sound and muttered, "I'm from nowhere. They found me under a rock." Seth laughed.

"You saying you're from Iraq?" Seth giggled.

Ms. Santana stared over her glasses. "Jacob and Seth, please…" She stood silently for a few seconds, radiating disapproval. "That means children are blends of their parents and their grandparents and all the people who came before them. For instance, my mother's family is from Ireland and my father's is from Mexico. People arrived here at different times, some seeking religious freedom or work or education, some enslaved. We have so many different histories and identities. This is part of our heritage."

Mohammed shifted uneasily in his seat. *I already struck out on the name thing. How can I share anything about my family?*

It's not that I'm ashamed really, but what would they think about living in a tent or having goats?

Noah gave him a friendly look. He slipped him a wrinkled piece of paper. TOFU MEET HUMMUS. Mohammed stared at the words and the fireworks scribbled next to it.

The last thing in the world Mohammed wanted to do was tell his classmates about his grandmother. *The weird food. The weird names. Living in a cave.* He could just imagine what Jacob would do with that.

Ms. Santana continued, "Can someone tell me, what is a family tree? Emily?"

"It's like when you draw a tree and you put the names of all your relatives on the different branches, and the grandfather and grandmother are the trunk."

"That's pretty close. Each family is a new branch. I'll give you a pattern and show you how to fill in the names, each generation of parents and children. There are lots of different kinds of families, so I want you to include everyone who is related to you in any way." She glanced around the class, making sure there were no questions. "Then I want you to make a list of five words that describe who you are, like brother, granddaughter, soccer player, Somali, red head. Think about what makes you feel proud."

She started handing out sheets of paper with the family tree and the assignment questions. Mohammed looked at the tree and the blank spaces. *Who am I? What am I proud of? I don't even know where I am from. Boston? Bethlehem? Nattif? How can I explain things that I don't really understand?* He felt a clutch in his throat. His mother called that feeling, confusalated.

Well I am so confusalated, maybe its bathroom pass time.

Noah watched him with a curious look on his face. He whispered, "You feeling like a freak? I can help you figure this out. My mother came from very far away too, with lots of relatives with really strange names."

Mohammed nodded and let out a deep breath that sounded like a giant whoosh of relief.

At recess, Noah showed Mohammed his Pokemon cards. "I just love collecting them, especially Dragon cards," Noah said proudly.

"Man, that's impressive," said Mohammed. "But, like where's your mother from?" All he could think of was somewhere with samurai and chopsticks.

"It's a long story," answered Noah.

Have hope you dope, Mohammed thought. "Okay, I got time. But I could sure use more energy cards now."

Chapter Seventeen

Rocks Or Wings

After school, Mohammed ran home, a new Pokemon card in his pocket, ready to add to his growing collection. *What am I going to do about this stupid research project? At least Noah thinks he can help me.* He walked into the kitchen where Sitti was cooking and said, "Do you have time now?"

Sitti was baking cheesy manakish, her version of pizza, and mixing vinegar and garlic to make pickles. Her hands were coated with flour from kneading the soft dough, sprinkling it with olive oil. Mohammed watched her heaping the zata'ar and patting it on each circle of dough with thin slices of white Nabulsy cheese. Sitti laughed, kissed his forehead and stared for a moment at his check. She slid the pans into the oven.

Mohammed turned suddenly when he heard Zaynab's loud voice coming from his parent's bedroom. "But mom, what am I gonna do?" Mohammed strode out of the kitchen, through the living room, and pushed the bedroom door open. He saw Zaynab, waving her arms dramatically, as she plopped on the double bed.

"Honey, I am sure we can talk with your principal and figure this out," her mother said calmly.

Oh, another drama with the family drama queen. I'm glad I can just wear… whatever.

"But mom, you just can't understand. You don't swim. You don't get what these kids are like. I'm talking about wearing a hijab during swim practice. I don't even know if I can and if I do, they'll look at me like I'm a freak or something."

"Zaynab, I think that tube cap and the hood look just fine. It's what a lot of Muslim girls wear these days. We saw it in the catalogue. And the swimsuit, well it just looks like, well, like a loose black wetsuit, like…you're going scuba diving."

"Mom, I'm NOT scuba diving, I'm trying out for the swim team. That's different. Get it? Besides, I don't even know if this school has any, what do they call it?"

"Accommodations. Accommodations for sports uniforms."

"I think I'm the first one to ask." Her eyes reddened. "I hate this stupid school." She stopped and stared at her shiny red toenails. "I don't have any allies here…like I did back home."

"I could be your ally," said Mohammed softly.

"Yeah right, a big help you would be."

"Zaynab, he's your brother, don't be so mean," said her mother.

Sitti called from the kitchen, "Mohammed, you wanted to talk? You too, Zaynab. I want you to hear my story. Our story."

"Our story? Right," snapped Zaynab. "I have enough trouble living in the 21st century."

Sitti walked to the bedroom door. "How can you know what to fight for if you don't know who you are? Or where you came from?"

Mohammed looked at his sister. "Come on Zaynab, let's listen to Sitti."

Zaynab harrumphed, got up, and followed them into the living room, dragging her feet against the carpet.

"Your battle scars are healing nicely." Sitti gave her flour dusted hands a quick wipe on the side of her apron. As they all sat down on the couch, she picked up her embroidery.

With the research project looming in his brain, Mohammed asked, "So what was it like for you, like when you were a girl?"

Sitti stopped a moment and said, "Well, as I told you, we didn't have running water or sinks with faucets or toilets."

"How did you wash your hair?" asked Zaynab, a mix of frustration and curiosity in her voice.

"I didn't. Not very often. My sisters and I had to walk down a long dusty road to a public water pump, we filled clay jugs and carried the water in the jugs balanced on our heads."

Mohammed stared at her. "On your head? You too? Did you do that in the morning, like before school?"

"Habibi, I only finished second grade. In fact, I never told you this, but I actually never learned to read except for a few basics like writing my name."

Zaynab stuck out her hand. "Wait. What? Sitti, why didn't you learn to read?"

"My family needed me at home, cooking, sewing, taking care of the younger children. I spent days working in the fields, planting eggplants and melons, harvesting olives."

Mohammed leaned towards his grandmother. *Sitti may not be able to read, but she sure remembers everything. And she even can tell what I'm thinking.* He called that, her "laser vision." Sitti was not sure what a laser was, but guessed it was a good thing.

"That's so…old fashioned, I mean for girls," said Zaynab.

"In my family, I collected the stories just like I collected the mint and the tomatoes. You can see, my head is filled with words and memories even if I can't write them down." Sitti laughed and exclaimed, "And believe me, I never forget."

"Sitti, you are like our own Wikipedia," said Mohammed, giving her a hug.

Sitti stopped embroidering and put her hands in her lap. The spool of thread dropped to the floor, rolling towards Mohammed like a strand of a spider's web, weaving him into her story.

She said quietly, "You know, everyone has a collection of things and memories, like the stuff in your backpack and your thoughts about your friends and your old school. Sometimes we carry these memories around and they weigh us down like rocks tied around our ankles, and sometimes they are like wings and they help us fly."

The smell of manakish drifted into the room. "Oh my, I don't want the dough to burn," Sitti exclaimed and rushed into the kitchen. "I'll be back in a minute."

Chapter Eighteen

Sitti's Story: Aida Refugee Camp, Bethlehem – 1967

Fatima awakens with the loud knocking on her door. She turns to Mohammed, "Who could that be? Haven't we had enough trouble? Go open the door."

Mohammed stretches and gets up grumbling, walking quietly down the stairs through the rooms the family has added over the last few years, past their sleeping children and his snoring parents. He unlocks the door cautiously with Fatima right behind him.

Layla stands there, her hair flying from her hastily thrown on scarf. "Let me in. *Jesh*, Israeli soldiers. They came looking for our brothers. Dalia's son Abdullah too," she says breathlessly.

"Come in. Who? Yusef? Bilal? Darweesh?"

"Bilal and Darweesh. You know they were at the protest last week. Aye, I'm in such a panic. What will happen?"

"This is exactly what I warned them about. Demonstrations end in arrests," Mohammed answers gruffly.

"Shhh, not now. You'll wake the children. Come into the kitchen and calm down. Have some tea. Tell us everything," says Fatima, bolting the door. She tries to steady her shaking hands.

She turns on the single light bulb over the kitchen table, boils water on the stove. "Sit, sit. Catch your breath."

Layla sinks into a chair and grips her hands together, trying to calm down.

Fatima hugs her. "Oh Layla. You look terrified. A few months ago, the sky was full of planes. It reminded me of 1948, the war all over again. Then the bombs started falling, and it all came back to me like it was yesterday. Hell on earth."

Layla says, "Except now the Israelis control everything."

Fatima pours the hot water into the metal tea pot and adds a sprig of sage.

"Who expected the war to be over in six days? Everything happened so quickly," says Layla.

Mohammed shakes his head and paces back and forth between the stove and a large sack of rice leaning against the wall. "Now the Israelis are saying, if you weren't here on the day of the census, you can't get ID papers. I'm worried for Dahlia and her family,"

"They fled to Jordan," added Fatima.

"It's ridiculous," replies Mohammed.

"But we stayed and now there is a price for that too," says Fatima bitterly, pouring the tea and scooping sugar into the cups.

Fatima touches her sister's shoulder gently, "But what just happened to you?"

Layla responds indignantly, "The Israelis chased us out of our homes once. We escaped in '48, but I refuse to do that again. They can kill us, but I will never run."

"But Layla, at what cost *this* time?" asks Mohammed.

"What happened?" demands Fatima.

Layla takes a deep breath and settles into her chair, staring at her tea. "It was maybe 2:00 in the morning, just two hours ago. The Israeli soldiers banged on our door and yelled. They broke down the door. The children screamed. I was frantic."

"Aye, pray for Allah's protection," Fatima responds, clutching her hands together.

"They yelled, 'Where's Bilal and Darweesh and Abdullah?' I didn't know. They said we were hiding guns."

"None of us ever touched a gun," exclaims Fatima.

"It was terrible. They called us dogs. They smashed the little furniture we have. They went into the kitchen, and…" She stops and sobs. "They turned everything upside down. Poured oil into sugar. Spilled the flour on the floor. Smashed the eggs…"

Fatima gets up and wraps her arms around her sister again. "Khalas, enough. Those bastards. Dear sister, try to stop shaking. Take a deep breath. You're okay."

"No, I'm not okay," Layla cries. "They beat Saeb with the butt of their guns. His head was bleeding, my poor husband. I was screaming, 'Leave him be. Leave him be. What harm has he done to you? Think of the children.'"

"Aye, what dogs *they* are," responds Fatima, holding her sister tight.

"They arrested him. I don't know where they took him or why." The tears stream down her face. "The children were hiding, wrapped in their blankets, crouching anywhere they could find. They heard the soldiers beat their father. THEIR FATHER…I couldn't stop them. I begged, I tried…" She starts wailing again, beating her chest.

Mohammed pulls out a cigarette, lights it slowly, and looks at her. "We have to stay calm. The soldiers are young kids. They don't know what they're doing."

Fatima glares at Mohammed and holds her sister fiercely. She feels a wave of rage rising up in her chest. "Aye, those Israelis," she mutters. "They call us terrorists? And brother Fadi, studying in Jerusalem. He too fled to Jordan. What is happening to our family? What will happen to us?"

Mohammed adds, "You saw Dalia and her husband. They were so angry and frightened they took their four youngest, loaded them into Thaher's truck, and drove east to Jordan."

"And now they may never be allowed back," Fatima says, shaking her head.

Omar appears in the doorway, rubbing the sleepiness from his eyes. "Mama, I heard you talking. You know the soldiers are mad about the general strike."

"Omar?"

"My friends, we've been demonstrating. When the soldiers come, we throw stones at them to make them go away."

Fatima looks at her son with alarm. "Omar, you will get yourself arrested."

Mohammed adds, "Or killed."

"But Baba, the teachers are striking, the shops are closed, we have to do something. Abdullah told me we can't rely on others for help. We have to resist the Israeli occupation, however we can."

"Son, I forbid you to do this. It's too dangerous."

"But Baba, before this war, we heard on the radio, the Arab armies will protect us. Did they? It's not enough to put a white flag on our roof. What has that done for us?" He glares at his father waiting for an answer.

There is a loud explosion, plates rattle, and concrete dust puffs through the house. All the children awaken, confused, and come running into the kitchen, screaming, "Mama, Baba."

Grandmother and Grandfather appear in the doorway, their bedclothes wrinkled and hastily wrapped around their bodies. "Pray for Allah's protection. What is going on?" says Grandfather. Fatima sees the old fear in his eyes.

Mohammed turns to his father. "The soldiers have come back into the camp. They arrested Saeb. It's another night raid. They're probably blowing up the house of someone they suspect of resistance."

"As usual, they act like animals and we are guilty until proven otherwise," adds Fatima twisting her wedding ring over and over and rocking back and forth.

"Layla, habibti, what happened?" asks Grandmother.

Layla gets up. "Ask Fatima. I have to get back to the children before anything else happens. I need to let Yusef know too. Pray for us and for Saeb." She adjusts her scarf and strides determinedly towards the door.

Omar says, "Auntie Layla, Abdullah says prayer is not enough. We have to resist the soldiers."

She turns to face him. "I am proud of both of you. You're only twelve, just be careful." She opens the door, scans the smoky neighborhood, and runs down the path, keeping in the shadows.

Allam runs to hug his brother. "Omar, my friends, we throw stones too. The soldiers, they don't scare me."

Mohammed turns to his sons. "They should. You don't know what you are doing. This is very risky. They have guns."

"I raised our sons not to be afraid. This is wrong. The soldiers, they don't understand that justice is on our side. Maybe they only understand stones. How can the world not see this?" asks Fatima.

"Fatima!" exclaims Mohammed, glaring at her.

There is a loud pounding on the door. "Open up!" yells a soldier. Fatima hears a jeep screeching to a stop in front of her house.

Chapter Nineteen

Belonging To What?

Mohammed startled when he heard Zaynab clearing her throat. *Was she crying?* She stood up, pressed her hand to her mouth as if she was about to explode, her eyes wide open.

"Sitti, why are you telling us this stuff?" she asked. "Isn't life hard enough now without remembering all this old misery?"

"Habibti, come sit."

"I'll stand."

"What happened at school?"

Zaynab just shook her head.

"Hey, are you crying?" asked Mohammed.

"Shut up, baby brother."

Sitti's face softened. "Habibti, kids can be so mean. Is that it? And wearing a hijab in America is not easy. I know. There is so much misunderstanding and hatred and…"

"Sitti, please, I know that."

"But you come from a strong family. Strong women too. And steadfast."

"Steadfast? Wadda you mean? " Zaynab whistled through her teeth, then shifted uneasily on her feet.

"My life in the village and in the refugee camp is now part of your life, like the feet you stand on. We need to live in the present, but we need to know the past as well. And understand our strength."

Zaynab straightened up. "But Sitti, I was born here. This is my home. How can I belong to something that didn't happen to me? I have enough trouble representing…" She stopped for a moment, then snapped in a snarky voice. "Representing the entire Arab world in my stupid school."

"Come sit," Sitti responded, patting the cushion beside her.

Mohammed tilted his head and said again, "Hey. Are you crying?"

Zaynab glared at him and reluctantly moved to perch on the arm of the couch, as far from Sitti as she could get.

"Something happened?" asked Sitti again, gently reaching to touch her arm.

Laser vision. Mohammed nodded his head.

Zaynab slumped dramatically onto the cushions beside Sitti. "Two somethings," she finally said and bit her lip. "I talked to the swim coach." Her eyes brimmed with tears. "And he said if I make the team…I, I have to wear a team suit, no accommodations. It's like I can be a swimmer or I can be a Muslim. It's sooo not fair." She grimaced. "Not fair!"

"Aye," said Sitti, shaking her head.

"So why even go to the tryouts?" Zaynab blew her nose on a tissue stuffed in her pocket. She took out a crumpled piece of paper, smoothed it open with the side of her hand, and handed it to Sitti. "And this."

Mohammed craned his neck to peer over Sitti's shoulder at the note.

His eyes bulged. OUR SCHOOL'S LITTLE TERRORIST! ISIS BOMBER! GO HOME.

"I can't do this," Zaynab said. "I can't wear the hijab at school. I'm like the one public Muslim in the whole place. And everyone hates me."

Mohammed nibbled on his finger nail. He felt anger rising in this chest and blushed a deep red. *Why would they hate my sister? For what she wears on her head?*

"And if I stop wearing the hijab, I'll feel like such a failure. I can't face Baba. He'll be so...so disappointed. And I really want to wear it, but..."

Sitti shook her head. "It is time we have a talk...with you, Mama, and Baba. The school too. We will figure this out together. This is not okay. Not in America."

Mohammed's thoughts swirled around the words: "Our school's little terrorist." He squirmed, unsure what to say to his sister, but impatient to hear more of the story Sitti was telling him before his sister exploded with all her real life drama.

He reached for Sitti's arm. "What happened when the soldiers came? What happened to Bilal and Darweesh and Abdullah? Tell me."

Zaynab leaned back and groaned, "Brothers. Doesn't anyone care about me?"

Chapter Twenty

Sitti's Story: Aida Camp, Bethlehem – 1981

N ext to the bus provided by the Red Cross for families of prisoners, Fatima and Mohammed wait outside the Al-Dhahiriya prison in Hebron. Fatima scans the concrete walls topped by ropes of barbed wire and the locked gates. She twists the edge of her loose sleeve and hunts for her fourteen-year-old son Tahir, searching for his big eyes and long-legged walk. She quietly prays to Allah. *He's just a child, just on the edge of growing up. Let there be mercy.* One by one, teenage boys with guarded expressions emerge from the imposing gates, eyes cautiously scanning the hundreds of gathered family members.

Will he be here? Is he hurt? Did they break his spirit? She rolls her prayer beads anxiously.

Fathers and older sons pace and smoke. The hours crawl by. Two Israeli soldiers lean against the metal gates chatting in Hebrew, their automatic weapons hanging loosely over their shoulders. They share an orange, dropping the peels on the ground.

Fatima cries, "Tahir." She runs to the boy and throws her arms around him, filled with so much emotion she is barely able to speak. "Oh, you look so skinny and you look taller, my sweet boy. We were so worried. Are you okay?"

She pulls him away and holds his shoulders, looking intently at his face as her eyes fill with tears. She touches a long pink scab down the side of his cheek and a bruise on his neck. "What is this? What did the soldiers do to you?"

Tahir looks down at his shoes and answers quietly, "They do it to everyone. It's nothing Mama."

Fatima kisses his face. *It's not nothing. Beating a fourteen-year-old boy.* She bites her lip, trying to control the trembling.

"Why couldn't I protect you when the soldiers came?" exclaims Mohammed, opening and closing his fists, his shoulders tense. He wraps his hands around Tahir's lanky arms.

"You couldn't, Baba. Nobody could."

No mother should see her child hurt like this. Bitterness rises in Fatima's throat.

Mohammed shakes his head, hugs his son, and kisses him three times back and forth on his cheeks. He frowns while eyeing the scar and the dark circles under the boy's eyes. Fatima notices Mohammed's look of rage and despair.

She walks towards the bus, one hand on Tahir's shoulder. She can feel her anger growing, spreading like a fire through her body, shooting down to the tips of her fingers. *Not here, the soldiers.* She swallows hard and her other hand grips the loose belt around her waist, her knuckles blanching. She stares at Mohammed as he lights another cigarette and inhales sharply, blowing the smoke out of tightly pursed lips.

They slide into the back of the waiting bus with Tahir wedged between his parents. Fatima relaxes and shakes her head as she feels the warmth of her son's leg against her own. Other families fill the empty seats. Fatima hears people chatting excitedly with their sons and an occasional daughter. She sees others without their children, crying or talking in low voices. Cigarette smoke drifts out the windows. The engine chokes and sputters, gathers strength, and starts down the hill on the journey home. Home to Bethlehem.

"When the soldiers dragged you into the jeep, I was so frightened," says Fatima.

"My goodness, it was the middle of the night, no warning," Mohammed adds.

"So many Israeli soldiers in the house. I can still hear them smashing down the door," says Fatima.

"Then we couldn't find you."

"The officials wouldn't tell us where you were. We searched for a good Israeli lawyer to manage your case," Mohammed adds.

"The lawyer said you were taken to Al-Moscobiyeh, just like Omar and your father six years ago," says Fatima.

"And then we found out they took you here to the prison in Hebron."

Tahir responds, "Baba, I know you tried to visit, the lawyer told me."

"Eleven weeks is a very long time," replies Mohammed. "I know."

"I really missed you, all my family." Tahir picks nervously at a blackened fingernail. Fatima sees the rim of tears in his eyes and senses the teenage swagger that is barely holding him together. His shirt has not been washed, and she smells the earthy odor of adolescent sweat and sees the grime in the creases of his hands.

"They wouldn't let me sleep. The bright lights. The same questions over and over."

"Did they feed you?"

"Hard bread, jam, fava beans."

"You hate fava beans," says Fatima, shaking her head.

Tahir snorts bitterly. "Rice, cold tea. No bathroom, just a stinky barrel in the room next to my bed, next to my food."

"Aye, the awful smells. My poor boy, how could you eat?"

"I couldn't." He stares past his mother, silently. She glances at his sharply defined collar bones poking out of his taut skin. "And there was always a soldier watching me. They said I was throwing stones, but Mama, you know I wasn't."

"I know."

"I tried not to answer their questions. 'Who was throwing stones? Name names.' The interrogations went on for hours. For days. Yelling at me. You know, they know everything. They hit me, over and over." His eyes finally overflow with tears. "They put a hood over my head. I couldn't breathe and they handcuffed me to a chair. The handcuff ties cut into my wrists. See, look."

Fatima gently takes his hands and traces her finger over the scabs and bruises on each wrist. "Habibi," she says kissing his wrists.

"Children should not have such scars. This is so crazy. If children don't throw stones, they get arrested. And if they do… what does the army expect? Children who have been yelled at going to school or tear gassed on the street or shot at. What do they think will happen? They will be angry. They will throw stones. It doesn't matter to the soldiers."

Mohammed adds grimly, "Damn them. We have stones. They have tanks and automatic weapons. Not a fair fight."

"They wanted me to be a collaborator, to spy on my family, to break any resistance in the camp."

"Son, they tried to destroy your spirit. You are young but you are brave. Now you are coming home."

Fatima hugs her son again. "I hope the military doesn't announce any more curfews or closures today. They happen more and more, anytime day or night."

"We get trapped in our houses or in the camp," says Mohammed.

"Our own prisons," Fatima nods. "May we get through the checkpoints today without any problems."

Tahir looks at his mother. "They told me they would come and arrest you, too." He grabs her hand tightly. "I was so frightened. But I had nothing to tell them. I don't know anything."

"Don't worry now," replies Mohammed, squeezing his son's hand. "You are with your Mama and your Baba."

"Aye, after his arrest, your brother Omar had nightmares and wet his bed for a year," Fatima says staring out of the bus window for a long moment.

The bus passes rows of twisted grapevines and olive trees rising in the distance on rolling, rocky brown hills. Fatima turns back to her son. "Hopefully it won't be so hard on you. Today your cousins will come over. I made you maqluba. After dinner, you can sleep in your own bed near your brothers."

"That will be good for you," says Mohammed.

The bus slows as they come to a checkpoint with a long line of cars. In front of them is a battered truck with two sheep in the back, bleating anxiously. Ahead of the truck, they see an ambulance and a pickup filled with tomatoes. Everyone in the bus grows silent. Hands reach for pockets and permits. The permits are passed forward to the driver. The bus inches forward. Fatima grabs Tahir's hand and bites her lip, quietly praying that nothing goes wrong. Stop, go, stop, go, stop, wait, go.

A young Israeli soldier a few years older than Tahir, wearing a large helmet and automatic weapon, appears at the driver's window. "IDs," he barks, scanning the passengers. The driver hands him the bundle of papers and everyone watches nervously. Finally, he hands them back and says, "Yalla, yalla, move."

As the bus lurches forward, passing the cluster of soldiers and the Israeli flag waving in the wind, a woman in the front seat starts passing out candies and everyone cheers and starts chatting and smiling.

Fatima's face brightens and she says, "Oh Tahir, I have good news. We got a letter from Omar, from America. He lives in a different world from us. Mohammed, you read it to him." For the first time, Tahir smiles and looks at his mother.

From his jacket pocket, Mohammed takes out a creased piece of paper scrawled with Arabic writing. Fatima notices that his hand is shaking. As he starts to read, his voice cracks. He coughs and tries to regain his composure.

Dear family,

I hope this letter reaches you and that you are safe. I am so thankful for the scholarship. You know I waited months for the permit to travel. The trip to Jordan for the visa was pretty uneventful, but not easy. You can't imagine the long, tedious wait and the lengthy inter-rogation at the Allenby Bridge to cross into Jordan. I was so afraid they would not let me leave. Traveling with the Jordanian passport was okay.

The plane flight was really amazing for a guy who has never left Palestine, but really long. I couldn't sleep. I was so excited and relieved.

The big frustration came when I arrived in Boston. The immigration official asked me where I was from and I said Beit Nattif, but (of course) he couldn't find it. He kept saying, "Palestine is not in my computer." He asked, "Do you mean Israel?" I explained to this guy that I am from the Aida Camp in Bethlehem, occupied by Jordan in 1948 and by Israel in 1967. My family is from the village of Nattif, located in Palestine, destroyed in 1948 by Israeli forces. The officer asked, "Then why do you have a Jordanian passport?" He didn't know anything. Does the world even know?

So…I explained that I was not a Jordanian citizen, I was a Palestinian refugee living in a camp under Israeli control, traveling with a Jordanian passport - the gov-ernment allows this since we do not have a state (yet). I had to show my university acceptance. He didn't believe I was going to be a graduate student. We went round and round, and then he just wrote "Israel" on my papers, stamped my forms, and I got into the country. Very strange. How could this immigration official say we do not exist? Our homes? Our history? Don't we walk on the same earth, just like him?

Baba, you will be pleased to know I have already signed up for courses at the university and rented a room in an apartment with four other students, two from India, one from Jordan, and one from somewhere in the south, I think Alabama. The English I studied back home feels like a different language here. Such different accents. I am getting better with practice.

It is so much easier living in Boston with no permits or curfews or closures. The water just runs out of the tap any time. Hot water. Amazing. Makes me feel clean and human. Like anything is possible. And you cannot imagine the size of the stores, always filled with so much food. So many shelves. So many choices. You wouldn't believe how many brands of cereal they make here. I will bring you lots of presents when I return. Tell me everything you want.

How are my brothers and sisters? I miss you all terribly. I am going to a meeting tonight at the Arab students' association, and I hope to meet others from our part of the world. I miss hearing Arabic. Mama, I really long for your cooking. I can't find good flat bread in this city, and no one has ever heard of maqluba. Maybe I will have to learn to cook. Anything is possible here.

Omar

"I want to go to America too, to study like Omar. I am sick of soldiers," Tahir says.

"Insha'allah," responds Fatima. "You must study hard for this."

Tahir stares out the window, looking at the big sky and open spaces. He takes a deep breath for the first time since he left the prison. Fatima feels his body relax. His jittery legs stop bouncing as he stretches them out a bit in the crowded bus.

The family arrives in Bethlehem and finds a taxi to Aida Camp. Tahir walks into his home and smiles at his brothers and sisters and the cluster of relatives sitting on the couch and folding chairs. Fatima rushes into the kitchen and emerges with a platter of sweets, followed by Dalal carrying small cups of thick Arabic coffee.

"Look at his face," Fatima states, pointing to her son. "Shameful."

"Mama. You saw them beat me that night."

"And put the blindfolds and handcuffs on."

"They hit my head again, I think with the butt of their guns, while I was in the jeep. During interrogation at the police station in Bethlehem, there was more beating. At the prison in Hebron too."

One cousin responds, "Man, they did that to me, too."

"Me, too," adds another, rolling up his pants leg to show his scars.

Tahir nods, "And the interrogations every day. Over and over."

Fatima stares at her son, a plate of food in her hand, as his story spills out. She says quietly, "They beat the boy out of you."

"They said, 'We saw you throw stones. Who else throws stones? We know what your father is planning.'" He shrugs, his eyebrows go up. "My father? That's ridiculous. There's more. They yelled, 'Are your uncles involved?'"

"Your father? Your uncles?" asks Fatima.

"Yes mama. 'Tell us. We will arrest your brother Ali, your sister Dalal. Name names. We know everyone's names. Then we'll let you go.'" Tahir stops and looks across the room at all of his family. He sits down on the couch, hugs his cousins and playfully punches their shoulders.

"Eat," says Fatima. "Praise be to Allah. Why are they doing this to us?"

"That is what they do," an uncle replies, sipping on his coffee. "That is just what they do."

FRIDAY

Chapter Twenty-One

Big Problem

O N Friday, after the math word problems, Ms. Santana announced, "Okay friends, we are going to continue working on our heritage assignment. Today I am asking you to pick an older family member and interview them for this project. Let's start with your questions."

Mia's hand shot up. "What if my grandparents aren't around?"

Ms. Santana replied, "Good question. Can you think of someone else who would know about your family history?"

"Like my mom?"

"Sure. Anyone else have ideas? Noah?"

"Like my uncle or my aunt?"

"Yes. You can even talk to cousins if they are older than you. Or an older person in your life who knows your family. What would you like to ask your interviewee? What do you think you would like to know?"

The class was quiet until Seth raised his hand. "What country my ancestors came from?" he asked.

"That's a good start," Ms. Santana replied. "The country, the city, the town. And if they do not know the country, then the continent. Can anyone name a continent?"

Seth responded, "Africa is a continent."

Noah added, "Antarctica and Asia."

Jacob yelled, "Argentinahhhh," and tipped back in his chair grinning. Seth and the back of the room boys laughed.

Ms. Santana said, "Jacob, inside voice and fourth-grade behavior, please. Is Argentina a continent?"

Jacob squirmed uncomfortably.

"Emily and Mia both yelled, "Argentina's a country." Mia giggled and added under her breath, "Doofus."

"Friends, what continent is Argentina located in?"

Amelia's hand popped up. "South America?"

"Excellent," Ms. Santana smiled. "What else would you like to know about your ancestors?"

Mohammed raised his hand. "What they ate?"

Noah suggested, "Their religion."

Jacob wondered, "What did they do for fun?"

Emily added "Why they came here and what clothes they wore."

Ms. Santana said, "Excellent ideas. Think about these suggestions. This afternoon together you will make a list to use for your interviews, but this is a good start. So now let's look at the map on the wall with all the continents and the different countries."

Everyone turned to look. Mohammed's eyes swept over the map. He spotted the Mediterranean Sea, Egypt, Israel, but he couldn't find Palestine.

I know it is somewhere near there. Where is it? Sitti talks about Palestine. Omar sent a letter to his family in Palestine. *Is it any different now?*

"Everyone is going to get a map, and we will be naming and coloring the countries that we are from," explained Ms. Santana.

Noah raised his hand, "I see China," he exclaimed excitedly.

Seth smiled and said, "And there is Africa."

Ms. Santana gave him a look.

"I mean the continent of Africa."

Emily pointed, "I see England and Ireland."

Mohammed cautiously raised his hand, "Where's Palestine?"

Jacob grunted, "Hey dude, I didn't know you were from Pakistan. Where's your turban, man? Hey, left your camel at home?"

Mohammed blushed a deep red and his stomach cramped up. He bit his nail. "It's Pa-les-tine," he said quietly. "P-A-L-E-S-T-I-N-E…And I don't have a camel," he added in a louder, angrier voice. Privately he added, *you salami jerk,* and snuck a look at Noah.

Ms. Santana stepped up to Jacob, "That is enough young man. I expect you to be a better thinker and a better listener. We are all learning about each other's families, and we will do that respectfully. Now stop and listen."

She wandered back to the front of the class with her fingers pressed against her forehead.

"Okay Noah, come up to the map and show the class where China is. Do you know what city your mom is from?"

Noah slid cautiously out of his seat. He knew how to find China but had no idea where in China his mother was from. He swept his finger over the map, pointing out the vast country that started at the China Sea. "That's where China is. That's all I know."

"Well, if you interview someone from the Chinese side of your family, you could ask about the city, right?" Noah nodded quietly, uneasy with all the attention. "Okay, now Mohammed, let's see if we can find Palestine."

Reluctantly, Mohammed crept up to the front of the class and turned to face the map. He easily located the Mediterranean Sea and then spotted Israel and Egypt. His eyes moved east and he came to Jordan, but no Palestine. North he spotted Lebanon and Syria. Ms. Santana stood behind him and asked, "Do you know if Palestine is a country?"

Mohammed replied, "My grandmother is from Palestine, so I know it is an actual place, and my dad says it should be a country, but I'm not really sure."

"Ahh," Ms. Santana responded gently. "Palestine isn't a country that is recognized by every other country. Plus, maps are always changing and sometimes they are out of date." Mohammed gave her a questioning look. "Sometimes there are countries that are struggling to be recognized. There are debates at the United Nations. There are wars, different opinions, which means the country may be missing from some maps or may not be official yet or may be involved in a political battle."

"Well how do I find it then?"

"What do you think?"

"Ask my grandmother?"

She looked at Mohammed and said, "That would be an excellent question for your grandmother."

She took a deep breath and looked at the class, her eyes moved back and forth to catch everyone's attention. "I am so excited we are learning about each other's families. This is going to be complicated, interesting, and fun, too. We are going to stretch our brains and our understanding.

"After your research, each student will take these little flags." She held up a packet of white flags with tacks at the base. "Write your name on each flag and mark all the places where your family members are from. It sounds like we all have a lot to learn."

Hmm, thought Mohammed, *I definitely need to talk to Sitti. I need some answers here. I gotta know! Now."*

Chapter Twenty-Two

Lunch Time Crime

Noah fist bumped Mohammed on the way to the cafeteria. "This is going to be my big day." He clutched his lunchbox, a little nervous, a little proud, a chopstick stuck behind each ear. Mohammed noticed the slight swagger in his step. Noah was turning some thoughts over in his mind. *Five things I am proud of. Okay here goes: soccer player, good friend, half Chinese, half Jewish - like from Poland...*he struggled for number five. *Funny? Maybe funny?* he wondered.

Noah thought about his mother making dough and chopping scallions and cabbage, mixing it all up with ground pork, and wrapping a spoonful of filling in a circle of dough, carefully pinching the top. He thought about the smell in the kitchen when she steamed the dumplings, how she said, "Baozi," with a musical sound so different from English. He thought about the cluster of baozi snuggled in his lunch box and all the lonely, forgotten lunches he hid in his locker and threw in the trash. Mohammed had told him about his grandmother's story. Noah knew how upset his mother would be if she realized the truth.

He inhaled quickly and exhaled long and hard, pressing his lips together. *Whooo. I guess I'll take this one bite at a time.* He laughed, thinking of marching through plates of baozi and egg custard, bite by bite.

"Hey, Mohammed, are you my partner in crime?" he joked. "The lunch time crime?" Mohammed laughed and imagined his falafel sandwich dripping with tahini sauce, wrapped in tin foil. He had made the balls of ground up chickpeas with Sitti last night, hands sticky with chickpea paste, tossing them into a skillet of hot oil. The balls danced and sizzled until they were crispy and fragrant with cumin and garlic, and a toasty brown color.

The two boys sat down laughing conspiratorially when Jacob snuck up behind them and peered over Mohammed's shoulder. "Looks like mud balls to me, but you towel heads eat weird food. And let's take a look at what your little Japanese buddy is eating."

Noah's back stiffened and his cheeks flushed. He turned around and pushed Jacob hard. "Just back off. I'm Chinese, don't you know anything? Leave us alone."

Jacob mocked in a whiney voice, "I'm Chineeeese, Leave us alone, leave us alone." He sat down at the end of the table, his legs spread across the bench like he was riding a bucking bronco. He tore open his sandwich and chomped into his salami. "Weirdos."

Mohammed stared at the salami. "Hey, you had salami yesterday and the day before. You have salami every day. What gives? Doesn't that get kinda boring? Doesn't your mom know how to cook?"

Jacob suddenly got fidgety and his face reddened, "Shut up."

Mohammed retorted firmly, "I said, why salami?"

There was a long pause as the two boys glared at Jacob. Suddenly he blurted out, "What do you care?" He stopped for a moment. "I don't have a mom, so get lost."

Mohammed sat up straight and his eyebrows shot towards the top of his forehead. "What? No mom?"

"Yeah, that's what I said, so stop asking before I punch you in the face."

Suddenly Mohammed felt concerned, his voice softened. "What happened to your mom?"

"None of your freakin' business."

Determined, Mohammed persisted. "No really, what happened?"

Jacob sneered, paused, and said dramatically, "She's dead. Satisfied now?"

Mohammed stopped for a minute, taking this information in. His mind was racing. "That's really…sad." He had so many questions running through his head, but all he could blurt out was, "Does your father know how to cook?"

Jacob glared at him, stood up, and stomped away. Mohammed recognized that look of hurt and loss in Jacob's eyes. He had seen this before. "Man, that's really messed up, maybe I shouldn't have said that." he told Noah.

Noah responded, "You're okay, but that was intense. No mom. Maybe that's why he's so angry all the time."

"Yeah. Angry that his mom died." Mohammed wondered if all this talk about families was just making Jacob feel worse and act worse too. *How can he ask his mom anything if she is dead, dead, dead?*

Chapter Twenty-Three

Rocks?

MOHAMMED WALKED HOME CRUNCHING HIS EYEBROWS TOGETHER, twirling his Frisbee. *What a week. Blistered feet. Outside toilets. Hungry children. Dead moms. Hateful hurting kids.* It was a lot to take in.

Are these memories like rocks or wings? He found Sitti sitting in her bedroom, staring at the open bottom drawer of her dresser. Zaynab sat next to her.

"Zaynab and I were just talking. Come here," said Sitti.

Mohammed looked into the dresser drawer, squatted, and picked up several folded scarves.

Zaynab took one of the blue scarves, the fringes were a bit tattered. "I'm gonna wear this one."

"Really, I thought you were giving up?" Mohammed asked.

Zaynab rolled her eyes and stared at him. "Baby brother, I talked with Baba and Mama, and Baba came to school today. We talked with my principal."

"What'd she say?"

"She was really nice. She said I'm not the only kid getting bullied."

"Another girl in a hijab?"

"No, silly, other things. Like there's this boy who's got a really bad stutter and he's totally tortured, mostly during lunch when the teachers aren't watching. And another girl who is really big and can barely run, you know she's got a big belly, and some of the kids are really cruel to her, like in gym."

"That's mean."

"The school counselors are trying to, you know, open kids' minds. They're planning…some new programs about…"

"About what?"

"About all the ways people are different. About respect and kindness. The principal said there's gonna be a new column in the school newspaper. I decided…I want to write for the paper, to talk about…"

"What happened to you?" Mohammed said.

"Yeah, and lots of ways to be a Muslim and stuff like that."

"Man, you are brave."

"And steadfast," Zaynab said with a smile and winked at Sitti.

"Zaynab, you know your father's determined, especially when it comes to his kids."

"Baba made an appointment with the swim coach. I don't know if he can change the guy's mind, but…"

Sitti interjected, "Your father said he thinks it's against the law."

"What law?" asked Mohammad.

"In this country, you can't make someone take off her hijab and wear a swim suit if it conflicts with her beliefs as a Muslim," Sitti replied.

"Yeah, he said it has to do with my civil rights. I googled it."

"What?"

"It's like the law is supposed to protect students from discrimination and Baba says that includes religion."

"Is he gonna sue the school?'

"Don't get all dramatic. He's going to talk with the coach. Just talk. So stay tuned baby bro."

"Like he might get a lawyer or something?" Mohammed asked again.

"Only if talking fails."

Looks like maybe the memories are wings after all. Mohammed put down the other scarfs and turned to the open drawer. Under the collection, he touched four brown paper packets of seeds.

"What are these?" asked Mohammed.

Sitti took the packets and quickly put them in her pocket. She rubbed her gold ring uneasily on her wrinkled finger. Her whole body shivered.

"Habibi, let me tell you another story first."

Chapter Twenty-Four

Sitti's Story: Aida Refugee Camp 1990

FATIMA LOOKS DOWN THE ROWS OF ANCIENT OLIVE TREES, admiring their thick, twisted trunks and silvery leaves. *This is the most beautiful classroom in the world.*

"Mama, keep your head down. Stay behind that tree," Hana says. "You really are too old for this. Remember we are close to the Jewish Israeli settlement of Gilo."

"My heart is young, sweetheart. Look, when I see the little children at the top of the grove sitting under that big olive tree with your sister Dalal, it makes me so proud," replies Fatima, adjusting her crouch.

"Listen to them reciting their alphabet and singing. And my daughter teaching." Fatima clutches her hands together and smiles. "She's teaching our history, Palestinian history."

"Oh, Mama."

"I am so glad you both went to the UN schools and then to university. Who could imagine the Israeli military order would close all the schools for two years? Now *you* are teaching our children under the trees."

"This Popular Education Campaign is the best resistance we have," answers Hana.

"Well my ideas changed a lot when the soldiers arrested Mohammed and Omar. I understand, we women are part of the struggle."

"Mama, that was over 20 years ago."

"They took my husband and my twelve-year-old boy, he was just a child. And they didn't release your father for six months, and there were never any charges."

"Of course, no charges. They had no evidence, not that that would stop them," says Hana.

"Omar came back after two weeks, a changed boy. You were only four, you don't remember much, but that changed me forever."

"Mama, I always remember your stories."

"Thanks be to Allah, Omar recovered from that terrible time. So many boys arrested since then, it's almost a normal part of being a child. And now, just imagine, he is in graduate school in, in…in the US. What's it called?"

"Boston."

"Ah yes, Boston. Engineering. I miss him so much, but I'm really glad he is not here now."

Fatima adds, "You remember how the soldiers came back? They beat your father several times in front of us, and my brothers Yusef and Bilal, too. You know they target the men, and of course there is your brother, Tahir."

"I will never forget what Tahir said to the soldiers when he got out of jail when they accused him of throwing stones. He's been arrested so many times. He was just fifteen, right?" Hana asks.

"Just fourteen."

"Right mama. He said, 'You stole my land, you put me in a refugee camp, you killed my friend. What do you want from me when I get out of jail. Should I hug you? Thank you?'"

"What a strong boy," Fatima says proudly. "But he worries me so. His temper may get him into more trouble."

"And we can't forget Uncle," adds Hana.

Fatima's eyes tear up, "Ah, Darweesh. It's now two years since the Israelis killed him. At home. In front of his children. For what? For what?" She throws her hands up. "He was a peaceful man. Now a martyr..." Fatima reaches over to touch her daughter's shoulder. "Enough of this," she says, shaking her head. "Enough of this suffering.

"As long as the Israeli military doesn't catch these kids studying here, we are good. You know, if we don't resist this occupation, we will go mad. Since I can't read, the least I can do is to be a lookout for soldiers..." Fatima wipes her eyes and shades them from the sun.

"Mama, just think, first the soldiers chased us out of the schools, then the churches and the mosques, then people's homes. So here we are, teaching under the sky. There's nothing left to demolish."

"This campaign," says Fatima.

Hana interrupts, "The Israelis can't stop us from educating our children. University students are happy to teach, even under the trees. It gives us a sense of purpose, a way to resist too, and children need to be educated."

"I am so glad we are part of it," says Fatima, blowing her nose and wiping her face with a wrinkled cotton handkerchief.

"I'm proud of you. At your age, hiding in an olive grove, watching for soldiers. We women are strong."

"The little kids will keep learning and be able to read and write," Fatima says.

"And the older kids will be ready for their national exams," adds Hana, "when this closure finally ends."

"I know, I know. Education is everything," Fatima smiles.

"No one is paying their taxes, the shops are closed, everyone's protesting. How long can this occupation go on?"

"And the daily marches, so many protesters," Fatima adds. "Did you see all the men who were arrested last week? Sitting cross-legged, blindfolded in the sun for hours, hands tied behind their backs…" She turns suddenly, her face frowning. "Listen. Do you hear that?"

Fatima peers through the trees down at the road and in the distance she sees two Israeli jeeps, loudspeakers blaring.

"THIS IS A MILITARY ORDER. YOU HAVE FIFTEEN MINUTES. YOU ARE UNDER CURFEW. RETURN TO YOUR HOMES AT ONCE OR YOU WILL BE ARRESTED OR SHOT. NOW! I REPEAT, THIS IS A MILITARY ORDER!"

"Mama. Quick. Go to Dalal," whispers Hana, glancing rapidly at the jeeps below.

"We must get to the children," says Fatima. She starts running up the hill, trips over a low rocky wall. "Aye, my ankle."

"Mama, do you need help?"

"No, no, keep moving." Fatima limps forward. "You take five kids back to your house, I'll take five to mine, and Dalal can take the rest down to Layla's. We have to get out of here."

They scramble up the hill. Hana scrapes her shin on an irregular stone in an unexpected ditch. "Ouch." She ducks around a cluster of olive trees to catch her breath as blood trickles down her shin into her shoe.

Fatima can feel her heart pounding, a crescent of sweat on her forehead dampens her hijab.

"Israeli soldiers. On the road." Hana yells at her sister as she reaches the top of the grove.

"Quick children, you, you, you. Follow my mother." Her blackboard clatters to the ground.

Soon Fatima and her two daughters take off, running in three directions, followed by lines of wide-eyed children, the little ones holding their hands outstretched. One little boy starts to cry, his brother hushes him with a shove, "Shut up. Run."

Fatima scrambles over stone walls, lifting each child up and down, past rolls of sharply coiled barbed wire. They reach the winding streets of the camp lined with blue metal doors, electrical wires criss crossed and dangling above. "Move quickly children."

A cloud of tear gas hangs in the air. One child starts to cough. The walls of the cinder block houses are pock marked with blackened bullet holes. At the end of the street, two young men, faces wrapped in keffiyehs, throw rocks at an oncoming Israeli tank.

"Watch out for the rocks on the street," Fatima yells. "Stay away from the tear gas canisters. Don't touch the bullet casings. Come, come along. Faster."

Breathing heavily as she gets to her house, her hands shake as she unlocks the door. She sees the Israeli jeep at the other end of the street. Soldiers in riot gear, guns pointing, leap from the jeep as she rapidly hustles the children into the house.

"Quick, go to the back of the house," she commands, locking the door. They run through the crowded living room into a back room with piles of mattresses and bags of grain. "Lie down, lie down. Keep your heads down. The bullets come through the windows."

The children know what to do, but the little boy starts to cry again. Fatima curls her aching body around him, adjusting her swollen ankle. "There, there, you are safe now." She kisses his thick curls and holds him tight as the others curl around her.

Bam, bam, bam. Bullets ricochet off walls, tires screech. She hears stones hitting metal, boys running, shouting in Hebrew and Arabic, cursing, a screech and then a loud shatter as the front window fractures into a thousand pieces.

"Aye, the window," Fatima mutters.

"I'm scared," a little girl screams. "Will we be shot?"

"There, there," comforts Fatima.

A loud tank roars past as tear gas drifts into the house. The children cough and whimper. One little girl wets her pants and calls, "Mama, Mama." Fatima rubs her back, singing softly, her heart racing.

"Sweethearts, we will wait here until it is quiet. Then I will get you some food. You must be scared and starving."

The little girl grabs Fatima's dress. "Noooo. Don't go."

"Don't worry habibti. I'll be careful. The kitchen is in the next room. I'll find you some dry clothes too."

"I'm hungry," says the little boy.

"I will get you all some bread. I think I have some hard-boiled eggs too. When the curfew is over, I'll bring you to your parents."

"How long will that be?" asks a little boy.

"I don't know," says Fatima. "Maybe a few hours." *Or a few days or even a few weeks,* she thinks. "You are safe with me. We will figure this out."

She hears the front door creak open and Mohammed and Tahir slip into the house and rush to the back room. Mohammed's arm is wrapped around his son's shoulders. Fatima can see that the young man's hand is wrapped in a keffiyeh, dripping with blood.

"Aye, my boy, you've been shot," gasps Fatima.

Chapter Twenty-Five

Sitti's Story:
Aida Refugee Camp – Spring 2000

FATIMA CLUTCHES THE LETTER FROM OMAR, RUBBING HER FINGER along the edge of the envelope. Wisps of gray hair curl over her forehead as she wipes the trickle of sweat running down her wrinkled cheeks. Her scarf hangs loosely over her shoulders. *What does it say? Oh, it is so much harder for me now that my beloved husband Mohammed has died, Allah Yirhamu, God grant him rest.* She looks around the living room, thin brown mattresses piled in a corner, a plump couch in the middle of the room, a picture of Al Aqsa Mosque taped to the wall. Framed photos of her husband in his younger days and her dead brother Darweesh sit on a side table next to a vase of faded plastic flowers.

I can read the faces of my children or the look of an Israeli soldier, but I can't read a letter. Fatima rubs her forehead in frustration. *Aye, that's what I need now.* "Where oh where did I put my glasses?" she asks no one in particular. *Thank goodness my girls are still here.* "Dalal. Where are you? Ah, the glasses."

"What is it mama?" Dalal appears from the kitchen, hands whitened with flour.

"Look, finally a letter from Omar." She slides the glasses up the bridge of her nose.

Dalal grabs the letter, sprinkling flour on her dark skirt. "Let me see." She sits on the couch and taps the cushion, motioning to her mother. "Sit. Sit." Two white fingerprints dust the dark upholstery.

"Read it slowly. I want to feel every line," Fatima says, lowering herself gently to the couch. "Aye," she sighs. "My back." She reaches for a strand of embroidery thread draped across the armrest.

Dalal takes a deep breath and slides her finger across the top of the envelope with a crackling as she rips open the paper.

Fatima twists and untwists the thread around her finger. The tip of her finger turns white, pink, then white again.

Dear Mama,

 I am sorry it has been so long since I was home for the funeral. It is difficult to get letters to the camp, and my engineering work has been very busy. Life in Boston is pretty good. As you know, the kids are growing up, Dima is already three, Marwa thinks she is so big now at five. The big news since our last phone call is that Ummayah and I are expecting our fourth baby. Zaynab just turned six and can't wait to meet her new brother. She mothers every baby, puppy, even turtle she meets. Ummayah jokes the baby will never learn to walk because Zaynab will insist on carrying him all the time.

 Marwa will be starting school in the fall. She is very interested in reading and knows her letters already. You would be so proud. I talk to Tahir by phone every week, and he has found friends and work in Detroit. His wife is expecting their second child.

 The main reason for this letter is that I am so worried about you staying at Aida Camp now that Father has passed. I hear from friends that tensions are increasing and some people are expecting an explosion of protests against the Israeli occupation. The Jewish settlements are growing and seizing more of our land, there is more Israeli military everywhere, more checkpoints, more incursions into the camp. You may wonder, why am I telling you this when you live it every day?

As your oldest son, I am writing you with a proposal. I want you to think about this carefully. Please come live with us in Boston. My children need to know you, and I want you to be part of our family, to taste your cooking, feel your love, celebrate Ramadan together, so many things I miss. A phone call every few months and a visit every few years is not enough. The calls are expensive for you and traveling with four children will be even more challenging. I know that Dalal is still living with you. With her teacher's salary she is able to support you, if she gets paid on time, but I worry about your safety and the hardships, not enough money, water, electricity, food. You are not getting any younger. What about your health? What if you are sick and you can't get to the hospital with all the roadblocks and checkpoints?

Our apartment has plenty of room. Ummayah totally supports my decision. Please take this invitation seriously. I will arrange the plane tickets and all the travel. All you need is the permit, which will take some effort, and we will take care of the rest.

We all send our love to the family.

Ebnakum al-Muklis, Your faithful son,

Omar

Dalal puts the letter down and turns to her mother. "Well?'

"Oh Dalal, I could never leave this place. My heart lives in every rock, in the smell of the earth, the blue of the sky, my dream of return. This is my home. You are here. And Mohammed is buried here. Hana and Seema and their families live in the camp. And my beloved olive trees give me so much joy.

"I understand mama, but life is like a book with many chapters. I think Omar misses you. You raised three tough daughters, we will be okay and we have work and lives here. The new baby is coming. Omar needs you to bring a piece of Palestine to Boston, and it sounds like they could use help with the kids. It has been almost 20 years. He wants his children to have roots, to know their sitti."

"But Palestine is in my blood, in the air I breathe, in my hopes to return to Nattif…"

"Mama, we always hope for return, but I doubt it's happening anytime soon."

"Aye, you are right. Not in my lifetime. I live on hopes and dreams….and fear. I have only been to Jordan once, never to the airport there. Never on an airplane." Sitti throws her hands up in the air and then thumps them into her lap. "It might crash. I could die. Aye, how could I ever leave? My feet have never left the ground."

"Mama, think of how difficult life has become. I cannot even visit friends outside the camp without standing in line for hours for a permit to travel and then sitting in a taxi at a roadblock or checkpoint after checkpoint. I never know if and when I will get home before some curfew is announced or some Israeli soldier starts yelling at me." Dalal waves the letter. "Mama, you're probably safer in an airplane."

Sitti gently strokes her daughter's face, nodding in cautious agreement.

"And what if you get sick? Like Omar said. What then? Sometimes people can't get through the checkpoints to get to the hospital. And the hospitals can't get supplies or the doctors get stuck at roadblocks and checkpoints. We live in a prison. You heard about that woman the other day. She delivered a baby at the checkpoint because the soldiers wouldn't let her pass. Imagine!"

Fatima nods. "They said she was fat." She gazes intently at her daughter.

"And the baby died, mama. The baby DIED."

Fatima unwraps the embroidery thread and drops it on the ground. She stares at the tangled pile of yarn, the tangled pieces of her life. She has lived so many chapters, what is next? Outside there is the plunking sound of rocks hitting metal, angry voices in Hebrew and Arabic, feet pounding on the path, the pop of gunfire, a scream. She hears a crowd gathering, a young man screaming, "The bullet. It got me. Mama, mama. Help me. Help me. I'm bleeding."

"Aye, another young man with a sling shot killed by another young man with a gun. When will it ever end?"

They both look up, hearing the distant wail of an ambulance.

"Okay Dalal, write this." She turns towards her daughter. "No, let's call. Let's tell him I'm coming."

Chapter Twenty-Six

Old Enough To Know

"Why didn't you tell me this stuff before?" Mohammed asked.

Sitti answered in a quiet, soft voice, "Habibi, this is hard to tell you. I wanted to protect you. I wanted you to be happy. I didn't want you to...to carry the burden of my sorrows as well as my victories."

"Oh Sitti." Zaynab rubbed her grandmother's shoulder gently.

"But now I think you are both old and strong enough. Mohammed, it's your birthday tomorrow. You are almost ten. Besides, you are asking me. Hard questions. And Zaynab too. The world is making you grow up too fast. I want you to be tough... like the thousand-year-old olive tree we loved in Nattif."

She took a deep breath and sighed. "Do you remember how many children I have?"

Mohammed thought about his uncles and aunts, some in America, some still "back home," some in a place called Jordan, and then so many, many cousins. He remembered the endless car rides to Newark and Detroit, all the fussing and kissing, and piles of sweets and food. He got to uncle number five and looked at Sitti hopefully.

"I think it's seven," replied Zaynab.

"Habayyeb, I had *ten* children, but three died as babies. Your father was number one, alhamdulillah. He studied very hard and went to Bethlehem University, in Palestine. I still remember the day he got the scholarship for graduate school and the morning I hugged him goodbye. He went off to a university in America. I couldn't even imagine such a place." Sitti inhaled deeply, staring at her hands, adrift in her thoughts.

"Sitti, is Palestine a country?" Mohammed asked seriously. "I couldn't find it on the map in school."

"Ah, that is a big question," Sitti replied. "For me, Palestine is a memory, a dream, a hope. It is a real place, an ancient place that has been fought over for many centuries."

"Yeah, but is it a country?"

"In 1948, after the war I told you about, most of Palestine was made into the country of Israel and the rest was taken over by Jordan and Egypt.

"Most of Palestine?" asked Mohammed.

"Yes. There were several wars between Israel and other Arab countries, but the war in 1967 was the most important for me."

Mohammed tried to wrap his brain around "several wars" and his peaceful, gray-haired sitti. *What else hasn't she told me?*

"In 1967 the Israeli military took control of the whole place. Since then there has been one struggle after another, trying to sort this all out. Trying to figure out who gets what."

"You mean, how does everyone ever live together?" asked Zaynab.

"Yes. And who's in charge? How do we share this land of Palestine?" Sitti shook her head and sighed.

"Is that why Israel, Jordan, and Egypt are on the map at school but not Palestine?" asked Mohammed.

"Yes, habibi. You should remember that Israel is a small but powerful country. Jewish people from all over the world have come to settle in Israel. They claim that this is their ancient home, and after all the killing in World War II, they deserve this home to keep themselves safe."

"But Sitti," interrupted Zaynab, "People like us are actually *from* all of Palestine, like in modern history. The part that was made into Israel and the part that now they're fighting over. That doesn't seem fair."

"Zaynab, you're right. It is not fair for us. But some Jews after the war, they needed a place to be safe and other countries wouldn't take them. Israelis thought if they grabbed the whole place just for themselves, that the world would look the other way."

"You mean like a bully that's a country?" asked Mohammed.

Sitti nodded. "And sadly, other countries mostly did nothing. Israel wants the land but doesn't want the people from that land. Like us. Like in 1948. But we have our dreams and our hopes and our rights, insha'allah."

"Dreams and hopes don't seem to cut it, Sitti," Zaynab replied.

Mohammed shook his head, still trying to wrap his brain around tanks and teargas and his grandmother.

"There were times of quiet in the camp, times when the Israeli soldiers and tanks invaded, and times when we resisted. People mostly fought back peacefully, but sometimes with guns and bombs, too."

"How did you fight back, Sitti? Did you have a gun?" Mohammed asked excitedly trying to imagine his sitti, ducking in a doorway, her finger on a trigger.

Sitti laughed, "No habibi, I have never even touched a gun. I fought back by refusing to give up, by always believing in my right to be there."

"Is that what you mean by 'rights?'" asked Zaynab.

Sitti nodded. "And there are international rights, legal rights. You should look that up too. In your google. There's lots of history."

"But Sitti, you said you fought back. How did you do that?" Mohammed wondered.

Sitti took a deep breath and said quietly, "Persistence. Patience. Samoud. We got up every morning, made breakfast, got everyone to school. When soldiers stopped us, we refused to turn back and waited in line. We argued. We ran when there were bullets flying, and we covered our faces when the air was filled with teargas." She paused for a moment, eyes moist.

"We harvested our olives and our apricots and lemons. We fasted during Ramadan and ate well during Eid Al-Fitr. We taught our children. We loved, we cried, we married, we had babies, we mourned our dead. We kept our dignity. That is how most Palestinians fought back."

Mohammed stopped and grew serious. For the first time he saw both a fierceness and a hardness in Sitti's eyes.

Mohammed asked, "Are you angry?"

Sitti threw her head back, closed her eyes. Her fists tightened. She took a deep breath and finally said, "Am I angry?" She stared at their faces for a moment and shook her head. "I lost my home, my childhood, sometimes even my hope. I lived a very hard life. Wouldn't you feel angry?"

Sitti stopped. "I am just lucky I had my family, my dreams, and my memories. All that kept me busy, gave me a life."

Mohammed nodded quietly, his eyes wide, intently watching Sitti.

Zaynab stood up. "I would be furious. In fact, I am furious!"

Sitti twisted her fingers together, rubbing her old ring. "It became a prison. The Israelis surrounded the camp with a huge concrete wall. A prison," she nodded her head.

"How could you stand it?" Zaynab stared directly at her grandmother.

Sitti turned to look straight at her. "My anger burns like a red flame in my heart. You should know, a refugee's life tastes of bitterness and despair, but that is not everything. I loved my husband and my children, the land and the life we made together." She stopped for a moment. "I refused to be destroyed."

Sitti exhaled a deep breath as if she had dumped a huge bucket of stones, harvested from the rocky soil around her family's old olive trees, right on Mohammed and Zaynab's feet. "Do you understand, habayyeh?"

Mohammed nodded again, searching his grandmother's eyes for the Sitti he was beginning to know.

"But life changes. The children grow up, they have children. Sedo, your grandfather, was fifteen years older than me, so he got old before I did. After he died, I couldn't stay there any longer. I got tired of all the suffering and your father invited me to America."

"But what happened to our families that stayed behind? I mean, now?" asked Zaynab, pacing back and forth.

"They are crowded together in our shrinking space and they continue to resist. The Israeli soldiers come into the camp night and day. The air is filled with teargas. But I need to spend my old age more peacefully near you and your family. I just…I need to breathe without choking."

Mohammed was a bit overwhelmed with all of this information. He spotted a seed packet poking out of Sitti's pocket. He started to feel inpatient. "Sitti, tell me about the packets of seeds, pleeease," he said, thumping his fingers on his thigh and biting his nail.

"They're important right? I mean if you don't want to talk about it, the seeds must mean something. Correcto?" said Zaynab. She turned to her brother. "Oh stop with the nail biting."

Mohammed shoved his hand under his leg.

Sitti exhaled slowly. She wrapped her arms around Mohammed and they snuggled into the couch. Zaynab sat, perched on the arm of the furniture. Sitti took another deep breath and Mohammed felt like he was being wrapped up in her story, cocooned in her scarves and her memories.

"I had a garden in the refugee camp. I grew tomatoes and cucumbers, mint and thyme. I worked the soil with my hands and fed my children from that garden. Every year I dried seeds in the sun and then planted them the next spring."

"You didn't go to a supermarket?" asked Mohammed.

"It was a poor refugee camp, dummy," Zaynab snapped.

Mohammed pushed Zaynab off the edge of the couch.

"Heh, I'm sitting here. Don't push me," She landed on the floor with a thump.

"Kids, please," Sitti said. "If there was something we didn't grow, there was a little market in the camp, but not much for food. When I came to America, I carried those packets of seeds onto the plane, hoping to plant *my* tomatoes and cucumbers, mint and thyme in the soil near my new home."

"But we never had a garden," said Zaynab, sitting on the rug, looking up at Sitti.

"Right, and your mama bought tomatoes in the supermarket, so these seeds had no place to grow."

Sitti took the seeds out of her pocket, passed Mohammed the little brown packets, and wrapped her gnarled hands around his soft fingers. He touched the folded brown paper and felt the strength of her grip.

Zaynab picked herself up and stared at the crinkled brown packets. She tucked a stray hair into her hijab, stood up extra tall, and smiled.

Mohammad reached for her hand. *Our home and Sitti's home, so different and so connected.*

Sitti said quietly, "Mohammed, for your birthday."

SATURDAY

Chapter Twenty-Seven

Our Birthday

THE NEXT DAY WAS SATURDAY, SEPTEMBER 9TH. "MY BIRTHDAY, my birthday," hummed Mohammed.

"Our birthday," whispered Sitti. When Mohammad galloped into the kitchen, he spotted a shiny new bike wrapped in a big red ribbon, a helium HAPPY BIRTHDAY!!! balloon tied to the handle bars, just like he had hoped.

"Yeeees, a new bike." He fist pumped the air. His mother kissed him on his head. She bustled around finishing the birthday cake, chocolate with chocolate fudge frosting, as Zaynab decorated the top with sugar frisbees, soccer balls, a bumpy, smiling iguana, and a row of black, white, and green flags with red triangles. His father stood on a ladder, hanging green and red streamers and balloons.

"I'll never have too much chocolate," said Mohammed grinning, sticking his finger in the bowl of leftover frosting.

His mother asked, "Birthday boy, is there anything else you want for your special day? Double digits. Birthday number ten is super important."

Mohammed pondered long and hard, his hand in his pocket wrapped around a small, smooth gold bracelet. *I am the same age as Sitti when she had fled from her village and walked and walked, blisters on her tired feet.* He had been figuring something out, something really important. His eyes twinkled.

Mohammed turned to his mother and said, "I know what else I want. I know about the old stone house and the olive trees and the goats and the garden in the refugee camp. I want to go there. Can we go to Sitti's home, to our...our other home? I want to go to Palestine." His mother gave him a quizzical look, smiled, and wrapped him in a hug.

"Of course habibi, of course we can. But honestly, this is both a wonderful and hard place to visit."

Mohammed looked at his mom, "But mom, I'm an American. Other kids travel all over the place. What's the problem?"

His mother sighed. "Yes, you are an American, but you are also a Palestinian. You know that Israeli soldiers control the whole area. Many cities are now surrounded by giant concrete walls with special terminals for entry and exit, including Bethlehem."

"I know that, Mom. Sitti told me," Mohammed said, his hands planted on his hips. "I'm ten, you know. I know stuff."

"I understand she has been telling you our stories. To get there we would have to take a long plane flight to Jordan and then spend hours waiting and answering questions from soldiers to even get across the border, as well as other checkpoints. But once we are there, it is such a beautiful place." Her eyes sparkled and she smiled. "I would love for you to meet your cousins and their families."

Mohammed beamed, "You know, Mama, I also want to visit the village of Nattif and see Sitti's old home, the one her father built."

His mother took another deep breath. "That is even more complicated because Nattif is now inside the country of Israel and we are not allowed to go there. Besides, the Israeli soldiers destroyed the village a long time ago."

"What? Why?" Mohammed gasped. *What's with the secrets in this family? Destroyed?*

"Because we are Palestinian and they wanted the land."

"Ohhh."

The doorbell rang and Mohammed looked at his mother intently, crunched his eyebrows together, and turned to run towards the front door to let his new friend Noah into the house.

"I am so glad you could come, Tofu," he smiled, glad for a distraction from all this heavy family stuff.

"Happy to be here, Mr. Mohammed Mohammed," Noah responded and flipped him a silver Frisbee wrapped in a blue ribbon.

Mohammed and Noah sauntered back into the kitchen, arms around each other's shoulders, grinning. Mohammed did a funny hopping dance because he was feeling so pleased. His brain was spinning with Sitti's and his mother's stories and the fact that his new friend Noah was actually standing in his kitchen. Sitti's kitchen.

"School world meet home world," he announced grinning.

His mother hugged him and nudged, "Introductions please."

"My mother, father, Sitti, my sisters Marwa, Dima, and Zaynab, meet my friend Tofu, I mean Noah."

Noah nodded, smiled, and shook everyone's hands. Then he popped off his hat and bowed dramatically. "Glad to meet you. Nǐ hǎo."

He winked at Mohammed, who did a quick shrug. "What are you doing? What was that you just said?"

Noah laughed, "That's Chinese for hello."

"Ohhh. Well then, as-salaam 'alaykum to you."

"What's with the flags on your cake?" asked Noah.

"Oh, they're Palestinian flags," said Zaynab. "We're from Palestine."

"Cool."

Mohammed laughed, stood extra tall, turned to Sitti and declared. "I have something for you too." She clasped her hands together and stared at him curiously. He reached into his pocket and handed her the torn, empty seed packets.

"What did you do with my seeds?" Sitti's lower lip trembled. "I trusted you to care for them. I trusted you to care for our story."

Noah followed as Mohammed wrapped his arms around his sitti and said, "Don't worry. Come into my room." He took her by the hand and together the three of them walked into the bedroom. They stepped over Marwa's stinky sneakers and Dima's scattered shirts. Along the sunny windowsill behind Zaynab's books was a row of clay pots with freshly potted soil, damp from watering, each carefully labeled in his very best handwriting:

TOMATOES

CUCUMBERS

MINT

THYME

Mohammed and Sitti stood quietly.

"Dude, are you a farmer? What's with the pots?" questioned Noah.

"These are gifts from my sitti. Ms. Santana might say these are my roots, Tofu, like these are my heritage," beamed Mohammed. "The seeds are from her garden, you know, from Palestine, from the refugee camp." Mohammed stopped and felt suddenly serious. "From my other home."

Sitti smiled with a twinkle and a tear in her eye. "Alhamdu-lillah," she said quietly to herself. "The boy's got wings."

Zaynab walked quietly into the room, her hands tucked in her jeans, wearing a faded blue hijab with ragged fringes, held tight with a sparkling pin. She put her arms around her grandmother and smiled. "We got samoud, Sitti."

"Steadfast and proud," added Mohammed. "Sitti, maybe you never planted those seeds in the garden, but you definitely planted them in me."

Glossary:

words to know

THIS IS A BOOK ABOUT A PALESTINIAN AMERICAN BOY who speaks English, his teenage sister, and his mother and grandmother who speak English and Arabic. He has a friend whose mother is Chinese. Here are some Arabic and Chinese words that will help you understand the story:

Abu: Father of

Alhamdulillah: Praise be to Allah (God)

As-salaam 'alaykum: Peace be upon you, common greeting

Baozi: Chinese, steamed dumplings

Binti: Daughter

Eid al Fitr: Celebration at the end of Ramadan

Freekeh: Green wheat that has been toasted and cracked

Habibi: Sweetheart or darling (for a boy)

Habibti: Sweetheart or darling (for a girl)

Habayyeb: Sweethearts or darlings (plural)

Hookah: Water pipe for smoking tobacco

Insha'allah: God willing

Khalas: An expression that means finished, done

Maqluba: Popular Palestinian dish with chicken or lamb, rice, and vegetables, served upside down

Manakish: Baked dough topped with thyme, cheese, or ground meat, like a pizza

Muezzin: A man who calls Muslims to prayer from a minaret in a mosque

Mulokhiya: Bitter vegetable used to make broth

Nabulsi: From the city of Nablus in the West Bank, Palestine

Nǐ hǎo: Chinese, hello

Sedo: Grandfather

Shoo malak: What's wrong

Sitti: Grandmother

Srour: Happiness

Sumac: Tart lemony spice used in Middle Eastern cooking

Taboon: An inverted cone shaped clay or metal oven used to bake flatbread

Um: Mother of

Wa-alaykum salaam: And upon you peace, common response to the greeting, As-salaam 'alaykum

Yalla: Hurry up, get going

Yehudi: Jewish person

Za'atar: Spice made of toasted sesame seeds, dried thyme, oregano, sumac and coarse salt

Guide for parents and teachers

THIS IS A STORY THAT IS BOTH UNIVERSAL AND specific, for all the children of refugees displaced by war and political conflict, growing up in the United States, trying to fit in with their peers, and asking basic questions about identity and family: Who am I? Where do I come from? Where is my home? Why are my name, appearance, family customs, food, language, religion different from my peers? Every refugee or immigrant family faces the challenges of assimilating into the dominant culture and at the same time grounding the younger generation in their own specific history, legacy, and connection to a place that is now often lost. At the same time, for those of us who have already made our homes here, it is our responsibility to welcome each new child and to encourage curiosity and understanding for the most recent immigrants who are joining our richly diverse and changing multicultural society.

This book can open a discussion about different kinds of refugee children and their cultures and histories; it also can be read with a particular emphasis on the unique story of Palestinian Americans. In writing this story I chose to imagine a specific refugee family with a particular history that is not generally explored in children's historical fiction. These narratives blend together many interviews and accounts I have collected over two decades of listening and documenting the history of the people in Israel/Palestine. In the 1948 Arab/Israeli war, 750,000 Palestinians fled the area that was to become the State of Israel, and their villages and homes were largely destroyed by Israeli forces. Many people became refugees living in camps run by the United Nations in the West Bank, Gaza, Lebanon, Syria, and Jordan. The UN developed a relief agency (UNRWA) that initially provided tents and then one- to two-room concrete houses that gradually grew into crowded, sprawling refugee camps, as well as schools and medical facilities that exist today.

In this book, Mohammed and Zaynab's grandparents were originally from Nattif, a small agricultural village near Jerusalem. In 1948, when she was ten years old, their paternal grandmother, Fatima, fled with her family to the West Bank and lived in a refugee camp in Bethlehem. This area was under Jordanian control until the 1967 War, when the West Bank, East Jerusalem, Golan Heights, and Gaza were occupied by Israeli forces. Over time there were many UN resolutions, peace plans, repeated Israeli incursions, home demolitions, arrests, and both violent and mostly nonviolent Palestinian resistance to the occupation.

Fatima grew up in the Aida Refugee Camp, married, and had a family; her children attended UNRWA schools. Palestinian culture places a high value on education and, like many refugee children, her son Omar studied engineering at Bethlehem University. He moved to Boston to attend graduate school and ultimately settled there, married a woman also from the refugee camp, and had four children including Zaynab and Mohammed. After the death of her husband, the grandmother, Fatima, joined the family in Boston, arriving the day Mohammed was born.

This book chronicles the experiences of Mohammed Omar Mohammed Abu Srour, a nine-year-old boy who feels very American, but becomes aware on the first day of fourth grade in a new school in a new city that he and his family are different from his classmates when they question his strange name. His sixteen-year-old sister Zaynab wears a hijab at school, is faced with harassment from other students, and torn by her desire to fit in and be a "normal" American teenager and her aspiration to practice Islam the way her family practices.

Mohammed develops a relationship with a friend, Noah Bernstein, who has a Chinese mother and experience negotiating classroom tribulations and bullying. Zaynab is tough and defiant at school, smart and active on the track and swim teams, but demoralized by the stresses of her Islamophobic classmates and unsure she can handle wearing a hijab and being so publicly Muslim.

Through their relationship with their grandmother and the stories she shares, Mohammed and Zaynab learn the truth about their rich and troubled past, a village family uprooted by war and occupation, nurtured by a rich tradition of storytelling, cooking, and love and yearning for the land. Her memories provide Mohammed and Zaynab with a growing confidence and pride in family, a sense of place and dignity, and the self-assurance to negotiate the many hurdles they face.

Cune Press

Cune Press was founded in 1994 to publish thoughtful writing of public importance. Our name is derived from "cuneiform." (In Latin *cuni* means "wedge.")

In the ancient Near East the development of cuneiform script—simpler and more adaptable than hieroglyphics—enabled a large class of merchants and landowners to become literate. Clay tablets inscribed with wedge-shaped stylus marks made possible a broad inter-meshing of individual efforts in trade and commerce.

Cuneiform enabled scholarship to exist and art to flower, and created what historians define as the world's first civilization. When the Phoenicians developed their sound-based alphabet, they expressed it in cuneiform.

The idea of Cune Press is the democratization of learning, the faith that rarefied ideas, pulled from dusty pedestals and displayed in the streets, can transform the lives of ordinary people. And it is the conviction that ordinary people, trusted with the most precious gifts of civilization, will give our culture elasticity and depth—a necessity if we are to survive in a time of rapid change.

Books from Cune Press

 Aswat: Voices from a Small Planet (a series from Cune Press)

Looking Both Ways   Pauline Kaldas
Stage Warriors   Sarah Imes Borden
Stories My Father Told Me   Helen Zughaib & Elia Zughaib
Girl Fighters   Carolyn Han

 Syria Crossroads (a series from Cune Press)

Leaving Syria   Bill Dienst & Madi Williamson
Visit the Old City of Aleppo   Khaldoun Fansa
Stories My Father Told Me   Helen Zughaib, Elia Zughai
Steel & Silk   Sami Moubayed
The Road from Damascus   Scott C. Davis
A Pen of Damascus Steel   Ali Ferzat
White Carnations   Musa Rahum Abbas
The Dusk Visitor   Musa al-Halool
Jinwar and Other Stories   Alex Poppe

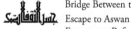 Bridge Between the Cultures (a series from Cune Press)

Escape to Aswan   Amal Sedky Winter
Empower a Refugee   Patricia Martin Holt
Muslims, Arabs & Arab Americans Nawar Shora
Afghanistan and Beyond   Linda Sartor
Music Has No Boundaries   Rafique Gangat
Apartheid Is a Crime   Mats Svensson
Curse of the Achille Lauro   Reem al-Nimer
Arab Boy Delivered   Paul A. Zarou
Confessions of a Knight Errant   Gretchen McCullough

WCW West Coast Writers

Fluid   Lisa Teasley
The Other Side of the Wall   Richard Hardigan
Kivu   Frederic Hunter
Finding Melody Sullivan   Alice Rothchild, MD
Joss, the Ambassador's Wife   Frederic Hunter
The Soldier, the Builder & the   Steven Schlesser
Diplomat

 Cune Cune Press: www.cunepress.com

ALICE ROTHCHILD is a physician, author, and filmmaker who loves storytelling that pushes boundaries and engages us in unexpected conversations. She practiced ob-gyn for almost 40 years and served as Assistant Professor of Obstetrics and Gynecology, Harvard Medical School. She writes and lectures widely, is the author of *Broken Promises, Broken Dreams: Stories of Jewish and Palestinian Trauma and Resilience* (translated into German and Hebrew); *On the Brink: Israel and Palestine on the Eve of the 2014 Gaza Invasion*; and *Condition Critical: Life and Death in Israel/Palestine* and she has contributed to a number of anthologies and poetry journals. She directed a documentary film, Voices Across the Divide and is a mentor for We Are Not Numbers, a program that supports young writers in Gaza. She received Boston Magazine's Best of Boston's Women Doctors Award, was named in Feminists Who Changed America 1963-1975, had her portrait painted for Robert Shetterly's Americans Who Tell the Truth, and was named a Peace Pioneer by the American Jewish Peace Archive.

Website www.alicerothchildbooks.com
Facebook https://www.facebook.com/alicerothchildmd
Twitter https://twitter.com/alicerothchild
Instagram https://www.instagram.com/alicerothchild/

Printed in the USA
CPSIA information can be obtained
at www.ICGtesting.com
JSHW012326281223
54480JS00003B/23